A Springful of Winters

Dawn Sister

Part of
SEASONS OF LOVE
Anthology

Beaten Track
www.beatentrackpublishing.com

A Springful of Winters

First published 2018 by Beaten Track Publishing
Copyright © 2018 Dawn Sister

All rights reserved.

ISBN: 978 1 78645 236 8

Cover Design: Steve Lancaster
https://www.facebook.com/weirdlybay

Beaten Track Publishing,
Burscough. Lancashire.
www.beatentrackpublishing.com

Acknowledgements

As always, there are people to thank. People who work tirelessly behind the scenes to make my scribblings into a professionally published book. People who answer my questions at three a.m. in the morning when I forget that they need sleep. People who sit and listen to me ranting about a difficult plot point I just can't work through. People who put up with my absent-mindedness and forgetfulness when my brain is focused on the story and not on real life.

To those people: thank you. Too numerous to mention, but all there for me when I need them.

A special mention must go to the person who designed the cover of this book. Steve, your doodles are epic.

Contents

Chapter One

It Shouldn't Snow in Spring
or
My Dog Isn't Trained Not to Crash Weddings

S NOW? ON THE first day of spring. It goes against all the rules of nature, Yenta." I huff as I look out the window of the bookshop where I work.

"Oh, come now, Kit," Yenta says in a soothing tone. "Even if it is the first day of spring, you have to admit, the snow looks beautiful. It's like Christmas again, or how Christmases used to be when I was a child."

"Christmas?" I exclaim, giving her a startled, disgusted look. "But it's nearly Easter. It's been winter for three flipping months. That was ample time to give us some snow, but nooooo, first day of spring and boom, it's bloody Snowmageddon out there. What the hell is going on?"

"In Russia, where I grew up, Lapushka, the snow would last well past Easter."

"Hmpf. That doesn't make me feel any happier. It's just wrong for it to be snowing when there should be sunshine and flowers. How will the daffodils grow now? I like daffodils. They can't grow if the ground is covered in snow. What if they don't come? What if the snow never goes? What if it stays winter forever, like Narnia when the White Witch made it forever winter and never Christmas? Or what if the winter lasts for decades like in Game of Thrones? It's the end of the world, Armageddon." I throw up

1

my hands in despair, pacing back and forth as I speak, watching my reflection in the glass.

I get distracted by the fact that I may not have brushed my hair this morning and it's falling in messy waves over my shoulder. I'm surprised Yenta didn't remind me. My eyes stand out, bright against the dark glass. I rarely look at myself in the mirror, so I am always surprised by how green they are. I stick out my tongue and then stop when I realise people passing by outside might wonder what I'm doing, a grown man staring at his reflection in the window and making faces.

"Lapushka." Yenta chuckles. "I think you may be overreacting. It is a late snowfall, and heavy, yes, but it is not the end of the world, I assure you. Come and have some tea. It is time to close the shop, anyway."

With a heavy sigh, I turn away from the front window and move to the door. I flip the closed sign over and push the bolt home. The bookshop has not been very busy today, mostly because of the snow.

I join Yenta on the comfy chairs in the window where our customers often sit and read. She pours the tea for us both.

Yenta is my boss and my landlady, since she owns the bookshop and the flat above, which is where I live. Most of all, though, she is my closest friend. She calls me *Lapushka*, even though my name is Kit. I don't mind her calling me that, because, apparently, in Russian it's some kind of term of endearment.

As always, there are cakes to go with the tea. Yenta likes to bake as well as own a bookshop, although I technically manage the shop, so she does have lots of time for baking. My stomach isn't complaining, anyway.

"The cakes are delicious, Yenta. As always."

"Thank you, Lapushka." She smiles as she takes a bite of hers.

This is our routine every weekday. Routines are good. Routines are safe. They make sense.

This routine is a way of winding down after work, and Yenta's way of thanking me even though I get paid—which is thanks enough—for being here and working for her. She is eighty. A spritely eighty, but she always says she could never have kept this shop going if it wasn't for me. I am just grateful that she gave me this chance after it seemed I would never get a job. No one wanted to employ me, even though I have two degrees, and I was in danger of becoming homeless and jobless when she stepped in and saved the day. A familiar sick feeling washes over me when I remember how close I was to losing everything. Including my mind. Two years and it's still difficult to even think about it.

Bessie, my beagle, slinks in, hoping for her walk to start early. She stays upstairs during the day but must have heard me throw the bolt home. She pushes her head up against my palm in greeting. It's her way of telling me she senses I'm upset about something, and she's there to ground me. I give her a grateful scratch behind her ears, and her tail thumps steadily on the floor as she accepts the attention.

I do overreact sometimes. Especially when things happen that I'm not expecting. I don't like change and I don't like when my routine gets interrupted. Snow certainly interrupts everyone's routine, especially when it is unexpected. So, to put it mildly, I'm not having a very good day.

"It was supposed to be sunny today. The weather app said it was going to be sunny. I'm never trusting that app again. The trouble is, I'm running out of weather apps to try. None of them seem to be one hundred percent accurate."

"Weather forecasting is not an exact science. The meteorologists do get it wrong sometimes."

"Hmpf."

To say I'm grumpy would be an understatement. "Why can't things just stay the same? It's the first day of spring, and this time last year, we had a glorious day…sunshine, warmth, lots of daffodils. This year, it's all gone to hell. And I have to walk Bessie in this."

"She will love it," Yenta tells me.

I shrug and sigh. "Yes, you're probably right. Judging by her behaviour this morning. She went absolutely crazy when I let her out in the yard. I've never seen dogs do the things she did. She rolled in snow, dug in it, buried herself in it. She ate it, Yenta. She ate the snow. At least it wasn't yellow." I grimace and shudder. "Or rather, it wasn't until she'd done her business."

Yenta is laughing, holding her sides. "Oh, I wish I could have seen that. She is a funny dog."

"She's a crazy dog." I chuckle. "She always does as she's told, though. I'm quite lucky in that respect."

"You will be all right walking her tonight?" Yenta asks. "You are not worried about the snow? You must wrap up very warm, of course."

"I've seen snow before, Yenta, just never at this time of year. I can cope with it, even if I have spent most of the day complaining about it."

She gives me a slightly admonishing look that says she's noticed I've spent all day complaining but really doesn't mind.

"It will most likely be gone tomorrow," she assures me. "And spring can begin in earnest."

"Hopefully." I'm not convinced.

"Where will you be going on your walk this evening?"

"It's Wednesday," I explain. "On Wednesdays, I walk Bessie in the woods."

"The track may be blocked."

"If it is, then I'll turn back and come back through the park."

"That sounds like a good plan, Lapushka."

With the plan settled, I take Bessie out for her walk.

I listen to Yenta's advice and put on warm layers. I've even put on a hat even though I hate wearing hats because they make my hair itch.

Most people don't get itchy hair. I do. I wish I didn't. It's a little difficult to explain how my hair can itch when strands of hair don't actually have any nerve endings. It's not my head that itches, though; it's definitely my hair. For the same reason, I don't get my hair cut very often. The last time I got it cut was two years ago. Yenta says it doesn't matter, that I suit long hair. That's just as well because if I could, I wouldn't ever get my hair cut again. The only reason I got it cut before was my mum made me, and after she died, it was my boyfriend, Harry. Then he left, so I didn't have to do what they said anymore. I miss my mum because she did more than just tell me what to do. I don't miss Harry because that's all he ever did.

Bessie behaves herself for the time it takes us to get to the woods and the track we usually take. This is mostly because the snow has been flattened down and frozen and she can't roll in it or dig it up. Once we reach the track, the snow is deeper, with even deeper drifts, and she goes completely bonkers again.

Like I told Yenta, I've never seen a dog do the things she's doing. Once I let her off the lead, she loses it. She jumps in the stuff, dives at it, like it's something alive for her to hunt. She's rolled in it so many times within the first five minutes, it's hard to tell if she's still a real dog or a snow dog. Her tail is wagging so fast there's a real chance she'll wag it off. She's utterly ridiculous about the entire thing and I don't think I've laughed so much in my life. I'm afraid I'm going to do myself an injury.

This continues throughout the woodland portion of our walk. The harder I laugh, the more outrageous she becomes. She is so wound up that when I call her to heel, for the first time since I got her, she doesn't come.

Thinking it was all part of our 'snow game', she waits until I get close enough to put the lead back on her collar, but before I manage to do it, she runs off again. She does this three times before I stop laughing. Things are beginning to get out of hand, and I start to panic.

"Bessie. Come here." I try to sound firm, commanding her the way I was taught at dog obedience classes, but it doesn't work. What am I going to do if she doesn't come? I can't leave her here, but I have to get home soon because Yenta is cooking dinner and she will worry if I'm not back.

I chase Bessie along the track as she runs from side to side chasing imaginary rabbits. I eventually catch up with her as she rolls enthusiastically in a patch of snow that does not look particularly white. In fact, it's not snow at all, because it is brown.

"Oh god, Bessie, I hope that's just mud."

My hopes are dashed when my nostrils are attacked by the familiar and most unwanted scent of fox excrement. This is a beagle trait, built into their genes by generations of her breed being used for fox hunting. Bessie is not a fox hunter, but she still rolls in fox poop whenever she finds it. I'm sure the bloody foxes leave it by the side of the track just for her…and to annoy me.

"Bessie!" I exclaim. "There is no way you are ever going to get anywhere near a fox, so why the hell do you roll in their crap?" I click my tongue as I fumble with the clip of her lead, trying, with frozen fingers, to attach it to her collar. "Now I'll have to bath you, and because you're such a mad dog, that means bathing me as well. Yenta won't have you anywhere near her house when you smell like this. Gah! You stink."

I'm getting increasingly worked up, cold, wet, and fucking annoyed, quite frankly.

Bessie decides that she needs to up her game because I haven't laughed for the last five minutes. So, instead of letting me clip the lead to her collar, she finds a hole in a fence that runs alongside this part of the track and disappears through it.

"Crap crappy crap crap!" I curse as I watch her squeeze her slightly puppy-plump body through the hole.

Beyond the fence is private land—belonging to a hotel, I think. I have no choice but to follow her, so we will both technically be trespassing. I hope the owner is understanding.

I can't fit through the hole Bessie wiggled through. I'm slim, but with four layers of warm clothes, there's no way I'm getting through there. I have to scale the fence.

I'm just glad there's no one around to see me fall on my face in the snow drift on the other side.

I get up and brush myself down just in time to see my wonderfully smelly dog disappear across the back lawn of the large mansion house hotel and in through an open door that's lit up like a beacon of welcome to a sociable beagle like Bessie.

I vent my utter frustration with a growled, "Fuuuuuuuck," before I set off in pursuit.

Judging by the flashing strobe lights and the noise emanating from the propped open fire door, there is a party going on in that very swank hotel. A party that has just been crashed by an overly friendly beagle covered in snow and fox poop.

I reach the door, out of breath and feeling the effort of running in my snow boots through freshly fallen, foot-deep snow. Peering inside, I gasp and feel the need to go off and hide somewhere on another planet—in another universe, maybe.

There is a woman…not just a woman. A bride, in a meringue-style white dress, except it's no longer white because there are two very obvious brown paw prints on the hem. She is holding a champagne flute, shouting and gesticulating wildly with her other hand and glaring in the direction that I assume Bessie has gone.

Shit, I hope she's already had her wedding photos taken because I am pretty sure that wedding insurance doesn't cover attacks from wild, shit-covered beagles.

I sneak in through the door, not really wanting to draw attention to the fact that I am responsible for this unfortunate mishap. I feel sick with panic now. When I make a plan, I like to try and include everything that might go wrong and list all the things I can do, or say, if those things do go wrong, but there's no way I could ever have predicted this would happen.

For a moment, I am frozen in indecision. Everyone is too busy consoling the hysterical bride so they didn't really notice me, which is just as well, because I'd rather have the floor open up and swallow me than have to talk to anyone right now. And right now, the possibility of the floor opening up is just as likely as the actual turn of events.

From my vantage point at the back of the room, I see Bessie weaving her way around the perimeter in stealth mode, heading towards the buffet. This is just getting worse and worse. I have to get to her before she gets to the food.

I can't go across the dance floor. I would attract too much attention, and I don't really want to face the wrath of an angry wedding party with an upset bride. I don't do interactions with people at the best of times, but angry people, I just can't deal with. Most of the time I don't even know what they're angry about, although it wouldn't take a degree in rocket science to work out the source of their anger tonight.

I edge around the room and exit via a side door. Surely there's a corridor running alongside this room. I can see other doors that lead off to somewhere. I can probably get to Bessie quicker going along the corridor than feeding through the party. My assumption is right, and once out in the corridor, I run.

I just get to the nearest door to the buffet section of the room when I am accosted by a member of staff—at least, I assume he is because he is wearing a waiter's uniform and carrying a bottle of champagne in an ice bucket.

"Can I help you? You look a bit lost." He's obviously taking in my appearance and realising I don't exactly fit the dress code for the night. I'm at a loss to think of a place I would fit in right now. I'm in such a state I must look like a wild man. "You can't be here, it's the staff access corridor. Are you invited to the party?"

He approaches me, and I feel my heart start to pump wildly. Words escape me, and I simply stare. That might have something to do with the fact that I am still out of breath after my run through the deep snow across the hotel lawn. It also has a lot to do with the fact that talking to people is not really one of my strong points, especially when I'm stressed. But my tongue-tied state might also be due to the fact that he is *fucking gorgeous*.

My eyes meet his perfect azure blue ones. It might still be winter outside, but it is definitely spring in here, because his eyes are like a clear spring morning. I don't usually notice people's eyes.

I avoid looking at them altogether because meeting someone's gaze is just too intimate, and overwhelming. It's like looking into someone's soul, and you can't do that when you first meet them. Eye contact is for close friends and family and something that happens after you get to know them very well, and I want to get to know this man. It's never going to happen, though, because he looks angry.

This tall, blonde Adonis in a crisp white shirt and black dress pants is hot as hell as he storms up to me, his blue eyes taking in my appearance and making judgements I don't want him to make, but in this situation, what else could possibly happen?

"What are you doing here?" he demands and I manage to hoarsely answer.

"M-my dog." I squeak. "She's in there." I grimace. "S-sorry!" He takes one startled look at me and then looks through the door, propped open with my foot.

"Holy shit! What's her name?" he asks, turning back to me.

"B-Bessie," I tell him.

"Stay there, I'll get her."

"Careful, she's covered in…oh." I'm too late to warn him about the fox poop because he's already through the door.

I try to shout the warning to him but the music is too loud and swallows my words, and it is already too late anyway. The Adonis that looks like spring has found Bessie and scooped her up in his arms. I see he has begun to realise the folly of his actions by the expression of disgust on his perfect face. His nose is wrinkled because there is no way he can ignore that smell.

I jump away from the doorway as he pushes backwards through it, turning his head from side to side to try to avoid Bessie's insistently friendly tongue.

"Here," he hisses urgently. "Take her and go, quick, before anyone sees you." He hands her over and I hesitate. Surely that can't be it. Surely I have to stay and face some sort of retribution for my part in this disaster.

"B-but the bride," I stutter. "Her dress. I should—"

"Her insurance will pay for it to be cleaned." Mr. Spring turns me and pushes me towards the main entrance. "You really don't want to go in there and try to explain. She's fucking bridezilla, and her family are all bonkers. They'll kill you. Literally. Go, before they come out here looking for you." His eyes sparkle, and I'm not sure if it's with mirth, or concern, or something else. I can never tell in the best of circumstances.

I do as he says. I really don't feel like getting murdered today, or any day. I don't dare look to see how dirty his shirt is. I don't even think I say thank you, the ungrateful sod that I am.

I get home without any more trouble and Bessie firmly on the lead. She looks as if she has had the best walk ever; I feel like I've been hit by a forty-ton truck.

After I've cleaned Bessie up as best I can, I go over to Yenta's house. She lives just across the back lane from her shop and flat. I tell her what happened over hot cocoa and crumpets, and I don't think I have seen her laugh so much. I'm glad my embarrassment has been such a good source of amusement.

Well, all right, thinking back it was kind of funny, but not while it was happening, and that waiter… I fancy my chances of ever seeing him again are pretty slim to non-existent, at least not unless I'm dreaming. I'm sure he will feature in my dreams tonight.

I know I should go over there and apologise, but I'm just a great big cowardly shithead when it comes to things like that, so yeah, not gonna happen.

Chapter Two

Finally Some Spring Weather
or
People Should Really Look Before
They Open Their Car Doors

THE SNOW LASTED two days. The worst two days of my life. Yenta has suffered more than me, however. Not only has she been stuck inside because she is eighty, and eighty-year-olds don't do well in icy conditions, even sprightly ones like her, but she has been stuck inside with me: an extremely grumpy twenty-four-year-old who hates having his routine disrupted by anything.

I like to keep fit. I go to the gym, and I cycle. I haven't been able to do either because the weather stopped me.

The weather has also prevented me from going over to apologise to that lovely waiter at the hotel. Apologise and perhaps check he didn't lose his job. Well, I'm using the weather as an excuse. I could have gone over, but I'm a coward, and things like this take time to plan. I can't just go over there and improvise. I have to think about what I'm going to say, write it all down, practise it all in front of the mirror, practise in front of Yenta. I know she's ready to throttle me because I've obsessed about this so much.

It's what I do when something is playing on my mind, and I won't get over it until I get it over with. He might turn out to be really nice and we can—urgh! I don't know—be friends maybe?

I am such a hopeless case. Who am I kidding? Even if I do pluck up the courage to go over there, he's going to see me at my most awkward and at best, accept my apology and send me packing. At worst, he'll call me something unpleasant and tell me to fuck off. People like him never want to get involved with people like me.

To take my mind off things, I go out on a bike ride. The shop closes half-day on a Saturday and the weather, though still cold, is dry with little trace of snow left anywhere.

Yenta takes Bessie home with her when we close the shop; I can't take a boisterous beagle on a bike ride, and she keeps Yenta company when I'm not around. I then get ready for my ride.

I always wear the same clothes. My cycling shorts are a little worn, but they're comfortable and familiar. I hate having to buy new things, and I'm fussy about what I wear, so when I find something I'm happy to wear, I tend to wear it out.

I always take the same route. I don't really mind riding different routes, but if I take the same one every time, I don't have to think about it. It means I can think of other things.

Other things like a good-looking waiter that I have nicknamed Mr. Spring because he has eyes like a clear blue spring sky.

It is because my mind is on 'other things' that I don't notice the car door open in front of my bike until it is almost too late.

With a cry, I slam on my breaks, stopping as my front wheel hits the open door. The bike overbalances and I fall sideways, straight into the lap of the driver of the car. Thank god for my helmet, otherwise my head would be in direct contact with this guy's, erm, helmet.

"Holy shit, are you all right?" the guy exclaims. "I didn't see you. I'm so sorry. Oh god…it's you."

"Bloody hell," I gasp, scrambling to get out of this guy's lap, except I'm wedged between the car, his lap and my bike. "Hasn't anyone ever told you to look before you open your door into oncoming traffic? I could've bloody broken my bloody neck." I don't really register his words until I utter the last 'bloody'. The situation is embarrassing enough without the lap belonging to Mr. bloody Spring. "Hoooo, shit." I give a half-sob, half-laugh of sheer embarrassment as I scramble unsuccessfully to stand up.

This is worse than Bessiegate. Far worse. I wish I had broken my neck now. Then at least I'd only have to face eternal damnation. A better option by far than facing him, like this.

"Hello again." Mr. Spring sounds as cheerful as his nickname suggests, and his eyes… Oh my god, they'd melt a frozen tundra.

"Um, hi?" I try to sound as casual as I can as I stop struggling, but it's not easy with my head in his lap and him acting as if we've just bumped into each other on the street.

"Hi." His smile gets broader, showing two rows of perfect teeth. "I was hoping I'd run into you again." He rolls his eyes and gives a low chuckle. "Well, not quite like this, obviously. Are you okay?"

"Er, what?" That eye-roll distracted me and his words kind of echo somewhere in the distance, drowned out by the bells I can hear. Is someone ringing bells? Maybe I hit my head and I have concussion. Did he just say he was hoping to run into me? Didn't I just run into him? "I'm not sure if I am all right, actually." When I'm embarrassed I get snippy and edgy and a little confrontational, all in an attempt to deflect from my utter humiliation. "Maybe that has something to do with the fact that someone who shall remain nameless thought it was a good idea to open their bloody car door without checking behind them first."

"Oh, well, sorry." He snorts. "I think I did apologise straight away but it bears saying again. Of course, while we're here laying blame, let's not forget one of the first things they tell you when you're doing your bikability at school is to watch out for arseholes who might open their car doors without looking behind them." He says this all with a smirk firmly in place, waiting for me to join in the joke. Well, if he thinks I'll let him off the hook that easily, he can think again, and also it gives me a perfect excuse to be angry with him and hide the fact that his smile, his eyes, his voice, his entire being melts me from the inside out.

He begins to help me to stand, pushing and lifting me from his lap. I bat away his hands in irritation.

"Thank you, I can manage," I hiss, pulling myself to my feet with as much dignity as a beached whale.

I smooth down my cycling shorts. Thank goodness they've managed to come out of this unscathed. I straighten and instantly regret standing so abruptly as a dizzy spell threatens to send me back into his lap.

I grab the open door as he jumps forward from his seat to support me, his hands on my hips, his head level with my crotch.

For a moment, time freezes and his eyes widen as he glances up at me through thick, blonde lashes. I find myself swallowing hard at the multitude of possibilities that are running through my head as I gaze into those spring-light eyes. Too much information, too much. I should look away but I don't want to. I don't think I've ever wanted anyone more than I have at this moment.

There must be some giveaway in my expression because his eyes widen even more and he pushes me gently away before letting go of my hips slowly, as if he is unsure of what he should do next.

Just when I thought this could not get any more embarrassing, my face heats to the boiling point of something metallic. If he was any closer I'd be in danger of melting his gold eyebrow stud.

"Erm, yes, well, sorry that I crashed into your car door," I stutter as I back off rapidly.

Without taking my eyes off him, I bend down to retrieve my bike and hear a telltale ripping sound as my threadbare bike shorts pick that moment to finally give up the ghost.

Oh my god, I'm going to die. The chain of my bike is jammed, and there's no way I can stop to fix it because my head is whirling. I now face a very awkward hike home with a broken bike and ripped shorts. When Mr. Spring opens his mouth—to point this out, I'm sure—I hold up my hand to stop him.

"Please don't," I say, not able to look him at him. "Don't look at me or even think about offering to help. I can manage."

"B-but your bike. And your shorts…" His breath hitches and I look up, startled.

"Are you laughing at me?" I glare angrily and he backs off, his hands up in defence, shaking his head.

"N-no. I wouldn't dream of it." He sounds a little less than genuine, and when my eyes narrow, he continues, his hands in a pleading position, "Truly, I'm not laughing at you. This is a terrible situation to be in, and some of it was my fault."

"Some of it?" I squeak, desperately trying to hold my ruined shorts together at the back.

"Well, all of it, because your shorts might not have, you know, if I hadn't, you know… At least let me offer you a lift home." He gestures towards the relative items as he speaks and he looks genuinely apologetic, but this is more than my low embarrassment threshold can take. I have to get out of here before my life starts flashing before my eyes and I expire from heat exposure.

"Look, thanks for the offer, but I don't think it's a good idea. I only live around the corner anyway." That's not true, but accepting a lift from a relative stranger was never part of my plan for today, nor was running into his car door. Things are beginning to get out of control, and I might have a bit of a hike to get home, but at least it will be along a route I know. Plus, the time it takes will give me the opportunity to reflect on how crazily embarrassing this has been.

"I'm sorry about the dog thing, you know? The other day. I hope you didn't lose your job or anything drastic like that." God, I sound like a right twat, but I have to get out of here, and because I doubt I am ever going to get another opportunity, I guess this is the best time to throw an apology at him and hope it sticks.

"Okay, that's no problem, mate." He frowns as he replies, obviously remembering how I'd just scarpered to let him take all the blame. "And I didn't lose my job, so no worries there either," he adds, still frowning as if he can't quite fathom me out.

He tips his head to one side, his blue eyes narrowed slightly and his brow furrowed so deeply I have the sudden urge to lick it.

Good god! I have to leave now.

"Oh, good, well, I'll be seeing you."

I'll be seeing you? I'll be bloody seeing you? Now I definitely sound like a twat. Why the hell would he ever want to see me again?

I turn and start to walk away as rapidly as I can with a buckled wheel and a bruised ego, not to mention torn shorts of which he now has an unobstructed view.

I turn with a gasp and start backing away, giving him a helpless pleading, pathetic look as I make another attempt to hold my ruined shorts together and retain the thin thread of dignity I have left. Dignity that has faded into myth.

Please stop watching me! Please get in your car and drive away. There's nothing to see here but a twat in ripped cycling shorts about to die of embarrassment.

He's biting his lip in an attempt not to laugh. I can see the laughter in his eyes, though, and I can't bear it. I don't care if he sees my arse, I need to leave now. I don't even stop when I hear him call out to me. I can't. I just can't deal with any more humiliation.

Chapter Three

Yenta Helps Me Make a Plan
or
Reading over People's Shoulders
Is Quite Rude Actually

WHEN I EVENTUALLY get home and manage to shower away some of the tension, I find a message from Yenta in her usual beautifully scripted handwriting:

> *Come over for dinner, Lapushka. I'm having roast chicken and I can't eat an entire bird on my own.*

I smile. She doesn't have to cook an entire chicken. She buys too much food because she knows I won't refuse to go and help her eat it.

I get ready and join her about half an hour later.

"You look tired, Lapushka," she comments as I kiss her forehead. She grabs my face and gives me an intense searching look.

"I've just had a five-mile hike with a buckled bike wheel," I admit. Knowing that she will demand no less than a full explanation and will know if I've left anything out, I tell her everything, from the car door opening to my less than dignified escape with ripped shorts.

When she finally stops laughing and wipes the tears from her eyes, she directs an admonishing look my way. "Oh, Lapushka.

You should perhaps have accepted his help. It would have saved you such a long walk home. Would it have been so bad?"

"Yenta!" I gasp. "Didn't you hear anything I've just said? I couldn't accept a lift from him. I mean, I abandoned him like a coward the first time we met and then never went back to apologise for mine, or Bessie's behaviour. Then I land in his lap and get all angry like it was entirely his fault when I'm really the one who should have been looking where I was going. Why would he even want to help me after such atrocious behaviour? He only offered out of politeness."

"And a wish to get to know you, perhaps, Lapushka?"

"To know me? What's there to know? I'm a grumpy grotbags and a coward to boot. He's probably back at home now, wherever that is, thanking his lucky stars I didn't accept."

"Nonsense, Lapushka. Sometimes I want to knock your head against something hard. Really." Yenta sounds angry. "You tell me that you wish to meet someone, but when you do, you do everything you can to push them away."

"I didn't meet him, Yenta. Bessie covered him in fox shit and almost cost him his job the first time. The second time, I landed in his lap and tried to blame the entire incident on him. Poor guy probably thinks I'm mad or that he's been run over by a steamroller. In fact, he might prefer that fate to ever getting to know me."

"You put yourself down so much. I don't understand. Anyone would be glad to know you, Lapushka."

I don't reply. I simply heave a sigh, blowing air out through my nose in a sort of derisive snort. Yenta says these things that I find very hard to accept. I think she sees a different me when she looks. I don't have any idea why because she's seen me at my very worst, when I get so anxious I can't even remember my own name. But she was there to help me when no one else was. She stayed when everyone else disappeared into the woodwork, never to reappear, including my boyfriend at the time. She's allowed to think what she wants and say what she wants, and there is nothing I wouldn't do for her, including this idea she has that I need to get out there and meet new people.

I mean, it's not as if I don't ever want to have friends, or perhaps a boyfriend eventually. It's just that, for me, it takes a little more planning and a little more effort on the part of potential friends or partners. Sometimes it is easier to just be by myself, but that isn't always possible and just a little bit lonely, to be honest.

"You should apologise to him," she suggests, and I sense she is about to make this an order that she knows I will never refuse.

"I did that already," I remind her.

"I don't mean something you just threw at him while you were running away." She waves her finger at me. "I mean a proper apology, with flowers."

"Flowers? Yenta, flowers are for funerals."

"Okay, beer, then, or whatever you think a man would want as an apology from another man who likes him."

"Likes him?" I choke.

"Kit Winters." Yenta rarely calls me anything but Lapushka, and even more rarely uses my full name. I am in real trouble now. "Are you a man or a parrot?"

I want to say I'm a parrot, because then I could fly off and hide in a tree. Instead, I lower my eyes and shuffle my feet as I reply.

"I'm a man." I try not to sound like a sullen teenager, but I fail miserably. Yenta has this way of making me feel so much younger than I am. Sometimes it's irritating, but most of the time I'm happy to let her get on with it, grateful that someone still wants to mother me, even when I'm such a grumpy grotbags.

Okay, maybe I do need to stop calling myself names. I don't like it when anyone else does.

"So, now we've established you're a man..." Yenta continues, a thoughtful expression on her face. It's the look she gets when she's planning my next move, because I am obviously incapable of doing this, especially where Mr. Spring is concerned. "What you need to do and what you should have done two days ago, but couldn't because of the weather, is to go over to that hotel and apologise to him properly." She steps up to me and tips her head back to examine my face. She's quite a bit smaller than me, but she can still boss me about, like a—well, like a boss. "Brush this lovely dark hair," she tells me, pretending to smooth her hand over the messy waves. "And flutter those mysterious green eyes and see what happens next."

I ignore her flattery, not because I don't have all of those things she described, but because I don't believe they are as beautiful as she says.

"But I don't even know his name," I counter. "How can I go and ask for him if I don't know his name?"

"You know what he looks like."

"Like spring." I sigh, gasping when I realise I've said this out loud.

Yenta's eyes dance as her grin broadens. "What was that you were saying about not liking him?"

"Okay, okay, so yes, I like him. Or rather, I'm attracted to him... You know, Yenta, I'm not really comfortable discussing this with...with you."

"Why? Because I'm a woman? Because I'm old? Because I grew up in a generation where men loving men was considered not only wrong, but illegal?"

"Maybe all of those things?" I grimace because she's asked me too many questions at once. I can't process them all. Her eyes stop dancing and she fixes me with a steely gaze. Uh-oh, what did I say to make her look like that? "Er, I mean, you're not old. I've known people half your age that were old and doddery. You're not like that at all." I won't make the mistake of calling her spritely to her face. I did that once and regretted it, even though it is a true description. "And I don't really think of you as a woman."

"Really?" She raises her eyebrows as she folds her arms across her chest.

"Okay, that was probably the wrong thing to say." I grimace again and she sighs, shaking her head but resigned to my awkward apology. "You see, I'm no good at anything like this, Yenta. He'll think I'm an arse if he doesn't already. He already thinks I'm a twat."

"So what do you have to lose?"

I regard her helplessly. Does she have to have an answer for every objection I put forward? And why does she have to sound so reasonable, and by default make me sound so unreasonable?

"I notice that you do not deny I am a twat."

"Oh, stop it." She hushes me. "I'm not being unreasonable here, Lapushka. Go over there and apologise to him. If he kicks you to the kerb, at least you'll have tried."

"Oh god, do you think he might really kick me? He didn't look the violent type, but I'm not a very good judge."

"Lapushka, stop worrying and start planning your next move."

"Okay." I hiss, my hands over my ears as I begin to pace. "But I need to find out his name first. I-I can't just go in there and ask for him by description. What if they say they've never heard of him? Or tell me to get lost?"

"So find out his name beforehand. It won't be that hard to do."

"How?"

"I can't believe I have to even say this to someone of your generation." She huffs. "Ever heard of Google?"

"I can't just google him by description," I say in disgust. Yenta might be more knowledgeable than most eighty-year-olds, but she doesn't know everything, apparently. "The internet and Siri are not omnipotent, Yenta."

"No, but you can google the hotel where he works. Sometimes these websites have staff photos. Sometimes they have lists of employee names and job titles. Try that."

I sigh. I'm not going to get out of this. Yenta will not rest until I've exhausted every avenue trying to find this man and apologise to. If she has to, she will personally drag me by the ear into that hotel foyer and make me stand there while they parade every member of staff in front of me until I find my guy. Not *my* guy, obviously, but…urgh…I pinch the bridge of my nose.

"Okay. I'll search on Google tomorrow in my lunch break," I promise her.

"Got all your contingency plans in place?" she asks me before I leave for the night.

"Yes, Yenta." I smile as I reply. She always makes sure to remind me that I have plans in place for almost every possible outcome in a given situation. Well, all possible outcomes except Bessie crashing weddings or me landing in beautiful men's laps.

I suppose you might call them risk assessments, my contingency plans. They tell me what I can do if something doesn't go to plan. In any given situation, I have contingency plans covering expected and unexpected events, or as many as I can think of. They help to calm my anxiety and let me know what I can do if something goes wrong.

Because of a burglary a few months ago, I do not have a laptop right now and my phone is just a basic standby for the same reason. I could use the computer in the shop. Yenta wouldn't mind at all, but I wouldn't feel right using it for personal stuff, even if it was her idea to use Google.

The next day, I finish off my morning tasks, leave Yenta in charge of the shop and make my way to the library. The library is one of the few places I feel comfortable besides the shop or my own flat. No one expects you to talk in a library; no one tries to strike up unnecessary conversations. Small talk, Yenta calls it. I never could get the hang of it, so I avoid it as much as I can. For situations when I can't avoid it, I have a contingency plan that usually involves steering the conversation towards one of my safe subjects.

"Hello, Kit," the librarian—I can't remember her name— greets me cheerfully. I should know her name, I mean, we talk all the time about books. We're in the same business, almost, so we always talk shop, which suits me fine. It's a safe subject. She knows my name. I just never got around to asking hers. Or maybe I did and I've just forgotten. I'm not very good with names. Does she think I'm a twat as well? She never seems to be thinking that when I'm speaking to her, but then, I'm not that good at reading expressions unless they're really obvious ones.

"Er, hello, erm…" I smile, because Yenta says my smile always hides any awkwardness I might be feeling. The librarian smiles back. A good start. "I need to use the internet," I tell her, suddenly remembering to look at her name badge. Ah, there it is. "Angela, please."

Well, that was bloody awkward, but never mind. She continues to smile. I can't tell if it's a genuine one or a fixed one. All smiles look the same to me. But she gives me an internet log-on code and directs me to a free computer.

Computers are easier than people. They're pretty predictable and usually do what you want them to, and if they aren't doing what you want, there's usually an easy solution to the problem. They're pretty black and white, with no variables to worry about.

The Google screen loads up, I type in the name of Mr. Spring's hotel, The Cosy Casala, and wait. Nothing comes up with that name—well, nothing that is local anyway. Most of the suggestions want to direct me to timeshare properties in Spain. That can't be right. I frown at the screen. Maybe I spelled it wrong.

"There's two 'S's and two 'L's in Cassalla," a voice from behind me offers.

"Oh, thank you," I reply automatically as I type in the correct spelling. The image of the correct hotel appears at the top of the list. Humming with satisfaction, I lean back in my seat.

"You're welcome," the voice behind me says.

I frown. Is someone reading over my shoulder? That's a bit rude. I turn to give the nosey git a piece of my mind and swallow the words as my eyes meet Mr. Spring's. I jump out of my seat in shock.

"Hello again." He grins, his spring-light eyes dancing in the bright lights of the library.

I glance at the computer screen which still shows the evidence of my search. There is no way he is going to think I was looking up the name of his hotel for any other reason than to stalk him.

What other reason could I possibly have? I could splutter out a million excuses, but he'd know I was lying because people can usually tell when I am. Now what do I do? I don't have a plan for this.

I can almost hear Yenta saying, *Ask him his name, Lapushka. He's standing right in front of you.*

However, the part of my brain that is able to think rationally is frozen to a standstill because him turning up and reading over my shoulder was never a part of the plan I had made with Yenta. We didn't factor for this, therefore I have no idea what I'm supposed to say or do. If I could just phone Yenta and ask her, but how stupid is that going to look and sound?

Hello, Yenta, it's me. That guy I like, the one I've been obsessing over for the last three days, has just caught me stalking him online. Please could you tell me what to say and do now so that he doesn't think I'm a complete and utter creep? Preferably with pictures, because my brain is seizing up.

"Hey, are you okay?" Mr. Spring frowns. Is he angry? Concerned? Worried that I'm going to beat him to death with the computer keyboard? Not that I would, but I can never tell what people are thinking just by looking at their faces. Sometimes there's just too much information to process. Sometimes there isn't enough. Plus, when I'm anxious, I do things that most people find quite strange, like wringing my hands together, rocking back and forth from my heels to my toes and other things that help me to calm down. Some people find that intimidating and upsetting. I try not to do it, but sometimes I can't help it, like now, I'm flicking my fingers and biting my bottom lip.

Come on, Kit, this isn't that difficult. People speak to other people all the time. Just open your mouth and make words come out of it.

"You're not supposed to be here," I manage to blurt out, directing my words at the floor by his feet rather than at him. It is the completely wrong thing to say, obviously.

"What?" he asks. "This is a public library, mate. I thought anyone was allowed to come in here."

I chance a quick peek at his face. He's confused, I think, which is better than angry, but not by much. Maybe I can explain a bit better?

"No, no, I mean, I didn't have a contingency plan because I didn't expect you to be here while I was searching for you online."

"Eh?" He looks even more confused. "Why were you searching for me online?"

I want to look at his eyes, because they're the thing I noticed first about him, so I glance at them quickly before staring at the floor again. His bright-blue eyes are now clouded and narrowed, and his top lip is curled in disgust, or maybe just bewilderment?

Oh god, what do I do now? I think I need to explain myself a little better. I take some deep breaths and make a conscious effort to stop flicking my fingers like some crazed lunatic.

"I'm not a stalker," I say so quickly that the words all meld into one.

"No? I, er, didn't think…" He seems a bit lost for words, and I think I might have messed this up very badly. If only I'd had a contingency plan for this, but it hadn't even crossed my mind that he might show up here.

I do have a plan for getting out of awkward, stressful situations though: run, run, and don't stop until you get home. So I follow that.

I back away from him. Unfortunately, I back into one of those trolleys the librarians use to return books to the shelves. The trolley moves, taking me by surprise, then it gets stuck against the side of a row of shelves, turns and slides away from me so I do a sort of pirouette before falling sideways like a dying swan, pulling several books from the nearest shelf as I do. They fall to the floor around me with resounding, ominous thuds, and I wince as each one hits the floor. Now, not only Mr. Spring is regarding me as if I'm an alien, the entire population of the library is also looking.

I scramble to my feet and scarper before anyone can start accusing me of destroying books. Oh god, I'm never going to be able to come back in here ever again.

"Hey, wait!" Mr. Spring calls to me, but I pretend I haven't heard and pick up my pace. I do that sort of quick walk that people do when they cross the road and realise there's a car coming so they speed up but don't quite make it into a run. They always look ridiculous, so I must look a right prat too.

When I get out of the door I do start to run, hoping he hasn't followed me. I don't stop until I get back to the shop, only to realise that I left my backpack behind at the library.

Oh god. Everything I need is in that backpack: my notebooks with all my contingency plans, my special shaped pen, my phone, my wallet, my collection of shells, my cards.

"Yenta?" I call as I burst through the shop door. "Yenta, I did it again." I wheeze, beginning to hyperventilate.

"Lapushka?" Yenta is worried, and I don't want her to be, but I don't know how to stop her feeling that way when I'm feeling so out of control.

"M-my backpack." I gasp. "Mr. Spring," I manage to stutter out. "Stalker."

I start pacing, rubbing my hands together. I haven't felt this anxious in such a long time, but that's because everything has been so settled and normal, with no surprises or any stress. Yenta's seen me like this, but she shouldn't have to cope with it. She's not my mum. She's not Harry. Harry never used to be able to calm me down either. Mum always knew what to do, but she never told anyone else how and she never wrote it down, so when she died, I couldn't explain to anyone how they could help me. Many people just stare at me, avoid me, or leave me on my own. Sometimes they get frustrated and angry.

Is Yenta going to do that? Will this be the time she eventually says enough is enough and tells me she needs someone more stable to run her bookstore?

Oh god, I'm going to lose my job, all because I wanted to find out more about some guy who probably doesn't even want anything to do with me. He definitely won't want anything to do with me now.

"Sit down and take some deep breaths," Yenta urges me, although she doesn't touch me. She knows I can't bear to be touched when I'm in this state. Every sense is heightened—touch, hearing, taste, sight. Touching hurts. Listening hurts. Every bloody thing hurts. "Lapushka, please."

"That isn't my name." I sob, holding my hands over my face.

"I know, I'm sorry. Kit, please. Sit down. Tell me what happened. Let me help if I can." She points to a seat as she tries to calm me.

She shouldn't have to say she's sorry. She calls me Lapushka because she loves me, not because she doesn't know my name. I don't mind her calling me that. In fact, I like it. But when I'm like this, I snap and say things I don't mean.

"I'm Kit," I say, sitting in the seat she pointed at and rocking as I hug myself tightly. Sometimes I feel like I'll float away if something doesn't hold me down. Yenta knows this. She gets my blanket and wraps it around my shoulders. I pull it over my head and rock. Bessie appears from somewhere and pokes her head beneath the blanket to get as close to me as possible. "I'm Kit," I repeat. "But I don't mind you calling me Lapushka. I'm sorry I snapped at you, Yenta."

My voice is muffled but I know she can hear me.

"It's quite all right, Lapushka. Settle now. Bessie's here. I'll make us some tea and then, when you are calm, we can go back to the library for your backpack."

"No!" I lift my head and the blanket falls away so I can see her. "I can't go back there, not ever. I fell over and pulled some books off the shelf. Mr. Spring thinks I'm stalking him, and everyone was staring at me as if I'd done it on purpose. I didn't do it on purpose, I swear, Yenta."

"Of course you didn't," Yenta assures me. "And the librarians will know that, Lapushka. They know you and they know you wouldn't damage a book on purpose."

"No, no, never. But I'm still not going back."

"What about your backpack?"

I grimace. If I don't go back for my backpack, what will happen to it, to all my things? I can't start all over again. Some of those shells were collected when I was on holidays with Mum. I can't do that over again, and they wouldn't be the same shells anyway.

"Can't you go for it, Yenta?"

I know her answer even before she's taken a breath to reply. She looks after me, but at the same time, she makes sure I know how to look after myself. That includes doing things that I hate doing but have to do anyway. What this means is that at some point today, after discussing the contingency plan, I will be going back to collect my backpack.

This fact both thrills me and fills me with dread. I want my stuff, but I don't want to go back to the place where I was embarrassed and embarrassing.

Yenta leaves to tend to a customer in the shop. I take the opportunity to go over what has happened and reassure myself that everything will work out, eventually, I hope.

I left my backpack in the library. This is okay. I can go back and get it. I just have to write down all the things I need to do and say, and try and predict what others will say or do in response, so there's no big surprises.

As for what happened with Mr. Spring…I doubt I will have to do anything about that, because if he didn't think I was a complete loony before, he does now and I doubt I'll be seeing him anymore.

"Kit?" Yenta's gentle tone makes me jump. "Oops, sorry. Kit, there's someone here to see you. They have your backpack. I think it's the young man you told me about, judging by your description."

"Oh god!" I gasp, actually flapping my hands in front of my face like some maiden in a Jane Austin novel. "What's he doing here? How did he find out where I work, live, work?"

"Perhaps he followed you?"

"No, no." I shake my head. "I ran too fast. Left him in the library. He couldn't have…"

"Maybe he looked you up on Google?" she offers. "The way you were trying to do to find out about him."

"There's nothing about me to look up." I frown. How could he look something up if he didn't know anything about me?

"Perhaps he asked the librarians?"

"They don't know where I live," I say in confusion. "I've never told them."

"No, but you wrote down your address on your library card application," Yenta reminds me.

"Oh, of course." Why didn't I think of that?

"Come and meet him, Lapushka. He's waiting, and his name is Stephan, by the way."

"His name is Stephan, by the way," I repeat.

Yenta's eyebrows rise, and I bite my lip. "Sorry," I say, because repeating what people have said to me is something else I do when I'm anxious. I hope I don't do this when I finally speak to… Oh god, I've forgotten already. I'm so used to calling him Mr. Spring. "What's his name again?"

"Honestly, Kit. I just told you, it's Stephan, Stephan, Stephan. Write it down then you won't forget."

I immediately reach for my backpack, then stop. "I can't," I wail. "I left my bag at the library."

"And Stephan brought it back for you."

"Oh." Sometimes my brain doesn't think in linear; it thinks in circles and wobbly lines that criss-cross and get entangled with each other. It means I often remember the ending, or the beginning of something, but the middle part gets lost somewhere in the ether. It's why I have to do things in a certain order because if I forget a step or miss it out, I'm screwed. And new situations, like this one, where I haven't even begun to think about the order of events, have me in a complete and utter flap.

"Get out there and say hello to him. You know how to do that."

"Of course I do." I know how to greet someone. So I should be able to go out and speak to Mr. Spring without any problems.

I stand up and walk to the opening that leads into the shop. It has a curtain rather than a door. I slowly lift one edge away from the wooden frame and peer through.

There he is, Mr. Spring, as large as life standing in Yenta's shop, holding my backpack.

"Oh dear." I step back, breathing hard. "I can't do this. He saw me lose it in the library, and I don't just mean my backpack." I turn back to face her. "Don't make me, please, Yenta."

She turns me around. "He would not have made the effort to bring your backpack here if he did not want to meet you." She gives me a gentle push to encourage me through the curtain as I try to remember my 'hello' protocol.

"Hello again," Mr. Spring says as I enter the shop.

"Oh, I'm supposed to say that first." I scowl, then realise this is not what I should have said and immediately turn to leave again, except Yenta is standing in the doorway, her face stern, as she holds Bessie's collar with one hand and points in the direction of Mr. Spring with the other. All my exits are barred until I've spoken to him.

I turn to face him, surprised that he's stayed actually. First sign of any oddness from me and people don't usually hesitate to leave.

"You know I don't mind if you want to start again," Mr. Spring tells me. I suddenly feel much better. If he wants to start again, that's fine. We can start from the proper beginning.

"Okay, thanks," I say and disappear behind the curtain, much to Yenta's annoyance.

"Get back out there, Kit Winters," she hisses. "He came to see you, not to stand in the middle of a bookshop and be completely ignored."

"He wasn't completely ignored. You spoke to him." I know I shouldn't point out the obvious, but sometimes the words are out of my mouth before my brain can stop them.

"Oh, goodness me, get out there before I blow a fuse," Yenta tells me.

I've never really understood what this means, because humans don't have fuses like plugs do. I know it means to lose your temper. Why can't people just say that instead of inventing all these verbal images that have nothing to do with what is being said?

I don't want to think about that right now, so I put into place one of my first contingency plans I ever wrote: 'saying hello'.

"First, you say hello," I whisper. "Hello," I say out loud to the rather startled looking Mr. Spring. "Then you put out your hand to shake theirs."

I'm forced to look up to see why my hand isn't being shaken by his. I haven't put up my hand, that's why. I immediately rectify this, and then, as he shakes my hand, I make a conscious effort to smile and do my best not to make it seem false or sardonic. Sometimes people think I'm making fun of them when actually I'm just trying my best to fit in and I have an unfortunate tone of voice, or expression on my face, like right now.

"Am I doing this right?" I ask out loud. "I think I forgot to tell you my name."

"Would it help if I told you mine?" Mr. Spring asks, one eyebrow quirked.

"M-maybe." My voice shakes with anxiety. This is very close to going wrong again.

"My name's Stephan," Stephan tells me without any hint of irritation, a smile on his face that is making the spring light in his eyes dance about like fire fairies.

"I'm, er, Kit," I tell him. "Kit Winters, and I'm sorry for running away, sorry for stalking you online, sorry for being an arse when I rode into your car door, and most of all, I'm sorry that Bessie covered you in fox crap." I grimace. "I probably shouldn't have said crap, maybe poop would have been better. Of course, I could have said shit, but that's probably worse than crap. Excrement, is the correct term for it, but that sounds a bit formal and scientific when you're just making an apology."

"Yes, it does." Stephan is staring at me, his eyes wide and his mouth twitching. I'm not sure what he's thinking, but at least he doesn't look annoyed. Things seem to have got a bit awkward until he speaks again and doesn't look uncomfortable at all. "I brought your backpack."

He holds it up for me, and I take it, trying my best not to stare at the floor but finding it difficult to look at him, because then I'd get distracted by his eyes. I could lose myself in those eyes.

"Th-thank you. I shouldn't have left it. I shouldn't have run off. I'm sorry."

"Yes, you said that already. You have nothing to be sorry for, Kit. In fact, I really should have looked before I opened my car door yesterday. But I suppose if I had, then I wouldn't have met you again and I really did want to."

"You did?" I look up now, his words distracting me from my awkwardness. He looks like he's telling the truth. "But why would you want to meet me again after the things Bessie did at your hotel?"

At the sound of her name, Bessie eventually bursts through the curtain, having been restrained by Yenta too long. Stephan gives a cry of alarm and then laughs as Bessie makes a beeline for him and covers him with doggy kisses.

He crouches down to make a fuss of her.

"Careful, she'll try to sit on your..." My warning comes just a little too late, as Bessie does her usual trick of trying to sit on someone's knee regardless of the position they are sitting in. She's not a big dog, but she's heavy, and she and Stephan end up in a heap on the floor as Stephan overbalances and she takes this as an invitation to sit on his stomach instead.

"Oh god." I grab her collar. "She's usually so well behaved. Bessie, heel," I command. She immediately stops smothering

Stephan and comes to my side, pushing her head up against my palm.

"Wow." Stephan sits up, regarding me with what looks like respect. "She's well trained."

"Oh, yes." I shrug. "Except I didn't really train her. We got her from an agency that trains support dogs. She's my erm…" I grimace. I really didn't want to tell him anything like this in our first conversation. It could be our first and our last, so I want him to go away thinking positive things about me, not wondering at how much of a basket case I am.

"We went to obedience classes so I could learn how to look after her properly," I explain. "She is usually very good at staying by my side. She was over-excited about the snow, and our evening walk is when she can let off some steam and burn some energy. Unfortunately, all of that combined the other night, and you and that poor bride got the brunt of it. Was she very angry?"

"No." Stephan dismisses my worries, and then makes a face. "Well, okay, she was angry—livid, actually, and so were her family—but believe me, the things with your dog were not the worst things that happened that night. She was a bridezilla, you know what I mean? She already had two of the waitresses in tears over some trivial thing to do with a smudge on a glass. And the rest of her family weren't much better. I caught two of the bridesmaids having sex in the men's toilets. And a bloke had to be escorted off the premises for making a pass at the barman. The evening ended up with the entire wedding party having a free-for-all brawl in the car park. We had to call the police."

"Oh dear." I'm trying to keep up with everything he's telling me. "Sounds like you had a horrible night."

He nods. "Yes, and your dog here provided a much-needed bit of light relief." When I still don't smile, he continues, "You have to admit, it was kind of funny."

"Not for the bride. She probably spent a fortune on that dress."

"Oh, she did. Apparently, it was designer, and she'd already told just about everyone who would listen how much she'd spent before Bessie here decided to add her own design. We offered to get it cleaned for her, but she refused. Said she had insurance. Anyway, that's not the best part of the story." Stephan waits for me to catch up, or perhaps he's waiting for me to ask him what the best part is. I hope I don't leave it too long to respond. I'm not good at knowing when it's my turn to speak.

"Oh?" I ask.

"No." He snorts, shaking his head. "The next day, after they'd all left, we discovered the wedding dress had been left behind. When I called her to ask if she wanted it delivered to her house, because I really didn't want her or any of her family back in the hotel, she told me to just put it in the bin."

"Her dress?" I ask in shock.

"Yes. She said just put it in the bin. It's ruined. I'm getting another one."

"Another one, but it's a wedding dress. Why would she need another one? You only need to wear it once."

"I know." Stephan holds up his hands in a gesture that I interpret as him being completely baffled by the entire incident. "Don't even ask. I don't know. One of our domestics, his partner runs a dry-cleaning agency. They've taken the dress to be professionally cleaned, and then we're doing what we do with all lost property—we donate it to a charity that deals with LGBTQ homelessness."

"Oh, that's a good idea." I regard him with curiosity. "Do you get a lot of lost property, then?"

"Tons. Mostly things people have left behind by mistake and they call us and we send them on to them. But sometimes it's stuff that the owner either didn't need, wanted to get rid of, or just plain forgot they owned. I've had people deny they left valuable jewellery before, when we know it could only have been them." He shrugs. "Whatever they leave is the charity's gain in the end. It just isn't worth arguing with some people."

"I used to volunteer in a charity shop," I offer, because this is one of my safe subjects. "That's where I met Yenta. She owned the shop, see, and allowed the charity to use it rent free."

"And now you work here?" Stephan looks about, nodding. "Sweet. At least, I'm assuming you work here, although…" He frowns. "This is the address that the librarians gave. Maybe they didn't want to give out your home address."

"Oh, I live here too. Above the shop."

"That's handy." His smile is a little wider than I might expect, like I've said something really amazing, instead of just offered a boring fact about myself.

"Yes, it is, but no snow days when the weather is bad." I scowl. "Which I hated, because it snowed on the first day of spring. I mean, I hated the snow, not the fact that I didn't get a snow day. I wouldn't have wanted a snow day. I love working here. I'm not just saying that because Yenta is listening at the curtain, because she probably is." I bite my lip when I see his expression go blank. I've said too much again. "What I'm trying to say is, I don't like the snow interrupting spring. It's wrong."

"Forecast is for snow again tomorrow," Stephan offers, his voice sounding a little strained, as if he's emotional about something. His news makes me gasp.

"Oh no, not again."

"Long-term forecast looks like this spring is going to be full of mini winters. A springful of winters. Ha, that's funny."

"You know springful isn't a real word," I point out.

He grins, showing a row of white teeth against his pink lips. He's so colourful, all golden, sky-blue, white and pink. There is something going on in my stomach that I really don't understand, and I wish I could leave and ask Yenta, but I know that would be rude, and the sensation isn't unpleasant, just strange.

"Good on you for making the most of the good weather by going out on your bike yesterday."

Exercise is a safe subject for me.

"I like to stay fit. Yenta says we should all do as much exercise as we can to stay healthy. She's eighty and still really fit, so I suppose she's right. She also says we should all eat well. She likes to make sure I eat well." I stop, because I'm oversharing again. "You probably didn't need to know that."

"Have dinner with me." Stephan is staring at me with an unreadable expression on his face. "That's why I was hoping to bump into you again. I would have asked you out yesterday when you crashed into my car, but you left. And just now, at the library, when I saw you at the computer station, I couldn't believe my luck. Have dinner with me, Kit, please?"

I feel a little overwhelmed, and if it wasn't for Bessie pushing her head against my palm and grounding me, I'd have left by now.

"I-I don't know…"

"I know you don't know anything about me. I can tell you, but I don't want to overload you. You can ask me anything you want over dinner. You choose the place."

I bite my lip. "It's not that I don't want to accept, because I do. It's just that I need a bit of time to plan, er, I mean, think about it." I wait for him to laugh, but he doesn't. Instead he smiles again, bombarding my brain with all that colour once more.

Stephan's smile is wide, and his eyes shine with the light of a thousand spring mornings. He looks like one of those footballers that's just scored the best goal of his career and is about to start running about with his shirt pulled over his face. Oh dear, I hope he doesn't actually do that. There's not a lot of room for running in the shop and Yenta might not like that there's a torso on display in her bookshop. Apart from the ones on the covers of the books, that is.

"That's okay." He continues to smile, as if the thing is a permanent feature now and he will keep on smiling even when he's left the shop. "I don't mind waiting."

"You don't?" I ask in surprise. "I mean most people, they just want an answer straight away, and I can't always give one."

"You get asked out to dinner a lot then, do you?" His smile has turned into a smirk.

"No-no, that's not what I meant. I mean, I need time to answer any question I'm asked." *Way to make yourself sound like a special case, Kit.*

"That's fine. I said I can wait." Stephan heads me off, saving me the effort of another long explanation. "How about I give you my number and then you can call me." I look up in alarm. He bites his lip. "Okay, text me, then. Text me when you've made a decision, and Kit?"

"Yes, Stephan?"

"Will you let me know either way?"

"Either way?" I ask in confusion.

"If you want to go to dinner, or if you don't, let me know. Please don't leave me hanging."

"I-I'll text you either way," I repeat for him.

This seems to satisfy him and he stands, holding out his hand to shake mine, this time in a goodbye gesture. I shake it, trying to give him eye contact but worrying too much about it and ending up staring at his hands, which are lovely, but not as lovely as his eyes.

"It was nice to finally meet you properly, Kit." Stephan says, shocking me into leaving go of his hand which I think I've held for longer than I should.

"Nice to finally meet you properly." I grimace, because I've just done that parrot thing, almost. "Er, too." I add to make it seem like I'm using my own words and not his. "I mean, it's nice to finally meet you too."

Now he needs to go before things get more awkward. Not that they ever got past the first stages of awkward to begin with, but there's still time yet. Up until the moment he disappears out the door, I hold my breath, just to stop myself from saying anything stupid or repeating what he's said again.

I turn away from the door to go back and speak to Yenta when the door opens again and he returns, breathless. It's unexpected and completely throws me.

"What?" I snap, sounding rather ungracious. He looks taken aback, and I shake my head. "No, no, I mean, sorry. You startled me. Did you forget something?"

"Y-yes, I forgot to give you my number."

"Oh." I sigh. Thank goodness it's something I can help him with rather than him asking me something I won't be able to answer. "Here, I have some paper."

"I could just put it in your phone," he suggests.

"No, I need it written down. I won't remember if it's put straight into my phone, but if you write it in my contingency—er, I mean my notebook, then I'll remember I have to call you."

"Okay." He takes my contingency plan notebook from me, and too late I realise the title of this particular notebook is fully on display.

–Contingency plans for meeting people and making friends–

"Oh god." I pull it back and fold the front cover back so he can't see. "Sorry." I hope he didn't read it. His expression is indecipherable as he writes his number and his name on the blank page I present to him.

As he hands it back to me, he smiles, and his hand brushes mine, not softly, because that would make me jump. The touch is firm, and I realise he is closing his fingers around my hand to hold it.

"Call me—I mean, text me, please?" He meets my gaze and holds it.

I can't reply because it's all too much: his eyes, his hand on mine, the strange fluttering sensation in my stomach. It's sensory overload. I nod, swallowing hard and sweating with the effort to not do anything that might make me look odd. He gives my hand a firm squeeze before letting it go and running out of the shop.

Chapter Four

Jogging Accidents Need First-Aiders
or
Bessie Likes Fishing for Phones

So, Stephan seems like a nice young man." Yenta is trying to get me to talk about him. I know this only because she hasn't been very subtle about it at all.

She's already asked me sixteen direct questions relating to what Stephan and I talked about after The Library Fiasco two days ago. I know for a fact she was listening at the curtain and heard every word, so I haven't told her anything she doesn't already know.

"So, are you going to call him?" she asks.

"I told you, I need to think about it," I tell her, not turning around as I place a book up on a high shelf.

"Yes, well, don't think too long, Lapushka." She huffs as she ticks off items on an invoice whilst unpacking our latest delivery.

"He said I could take all the time I needed." I climb down from the ladder and stand in front of her.

"People say that, yes." She regards me over the top of her tiny glasses. "But what they actually mean is they would like you to call them at least the next day."

"I texted him as soon as he left the shop."

"A text to tell him you have his number, something he already knew, does not count." She picks up a pile of books and hands them to me.

"Then someone's rewriting the rules." I scowl, balancing the books on both arms and huffing and puffing as I take them to the next shelf along, moving the wheeled stepladder with my foot. "Why didn't he tell me how long he was willing to wait?"

"Because to him, that would have seemed like he was pushing you, and some people, they don't like to be pushy." Yenta shrugs. "He wants you to make the decision by yourself."

"Yes, and I will. And if he isn't willing to wait however long it takes me, then he isn't the one for me. And if he had a deadline in mind, then he should have said so."

Yenta comes to stand below the ladder as I climb it.

"Not everyone understands how your brain works, Lapushka."

"Huh, tell me about it." I read the title of the first book on my pile and place it in the correct spot on the shelf. I wave the next one at Yenta. "Sometimes I wish I could just write a manual and get everyone to read it. Like this Haynes manual except for me instead of a car."

"I would help you." She nods, strands of her grey hair falling across her face. "And I would buy ten copies, then I would translate it into Russian and German."

I laugh. "Of course you would, and you would hand out copies to everyone that passed by the shop and I wouldn't make any money from it."

"Would making money be your first priority, Lapushka? Really?"

"No." I watch her as she bends over the box of newly delivered books. "Having people understand me, and therefore, by happy chance, understand everyone else like me, that would be my goal."

"There is no one in the world like you, Kit. You are unique." Yenta directs her gaze at me, and for once I don't look away. I just roll my eyes.

"You know what I mean," I tell her, and she grins.

"Yes, yes, I do." She heaves a sigh, as if she is thinking some heavy thoughts. "Are you going to tell Stephan?"

I blow out my cheeks and watch her via her reflection in the window as I think.

"I know I should," I muse. "I mean, it would make things easier, for him, to understand I mean, but it always seems like I'm making a confession, and I haven't done anything wrong. I don't want him to think he has to do anything differently, but at the same time, I need him to understand that he might have to, you know, do some things differently. He probably does need to know that I'm a bit of an oddbod who occasionally goes off the rails quite spectacularly."

"You are not an oddbod. and you do not go 'off the rails'. You just get upset if something goes wrong with your contingency plans."

"Yes, yes, I know that, and you know that, but no one else does. Some people are just not willing to adjust the way they do things to accommodate. And it's not as if I'm asking for any special treatment, because I'm not. I just need more time to do some things."

"Stephan seemed to know that you needed to start over again, and he didn't mind."

For once, I can read her unsaid words as if I'm reading a book. "Yes, yes, I'll text him today after work. That doesn't mean that I'll be going on a date with him. People don't usually think a fast food outlet is the most appropriate setting for a first date."

"Tsh," Yenta hisses. "You do eat other foods, Lapushka."

"I know, I know, just not at restaurants. Too many people, too many smells."

"Maybe he will suggest something different."

"He said it was my choice, though."

"Yes, but perhaps he has made a contingency plan of his own."

"Why would he even do that?"

"Because he likes you? Perhaps you did not notice, but I saw the way he smiled at you, Lapushka. As if you were the world."

"As if I was the what? That's just nonsense, Yenta. Almost as nonsense as some of the stories in these books." I wave a hand in a wide arc to incorporate all of the romance section.

Yenta narrows her eyes and leans forward, poking a bony index finger at me. "The same nonsense that I see you reading every day, Lapushka, so don't pretend you don't know anything about romance."

"I read it. Doesn't mean I understand it," I mutter, feeling petulant that she's called me out on my 'nonsense'. "It's time for me to walk Bessie. Do you want me to get you anything on the way home?"

"No, no. You go. I will shut the shop and see you tomorrow, Lapushka. Have a nice evening."

A nice evening. It's spent all day snowing again. I can't believe we've just got rid of one lot of snow then another lot comes along. *A springful of winters*, was the way Stephan described it. And when I pointed out that 'springful' was not a real word, he laughed, but not in an unkind way. It was different, but not in a way I can describe yet.

I need more time to think. Yenta is right, though, I shouldn't keep him waiting. I want to call him, but I have trouble understanding when it's my turn to speak when I'm talking to someone face-to-face. I have absolutely no hope when it's just a voice on the other end of a phone connection.

I worry at my lip ring as Bessie and I walk towards the woodland track. It has been an entire week since Bessiegate. I have set routes that I walk with her. I would take her the same way every day, but Yenta says Bessie might get bored, so I have several routes in my dog-walking contingency plan. Today it is woodland day. Tomorrow we will go to the park.

The woodland track is slushy in some places and frozen in others. I don't like the disruption of snow when it's supposed to be springtime, but I still quite enjoy the phenomenon. I like the sound of ice cracking beneath my boots, and the way everything is muffled and echoey at the same time.

I like the feel of the cold on my cheeks, and when my ears get cold, I press my fingernails against them because it feels cool and soothing.

No one else understands why I do things like that. Stephan isn't going to either, yet…

The world, Yenta said.

The part of my brain that interprets everything literally wants to scream out that I look nothing like the world. The other part, the part that enjoys reading romance novels and dreaming of happy endings wants to curl up in his lap and let him shower me with silly metaphors like that, forever.

I should just call him. Right now. Without thinking about it. I mean, without thinking about it any more, because I have done nothing but think about what he asked for two whole days. I have already come up with a plan that may be acceptable to him as well as me. I don't like eating out, but I can cook. I don't like going to new places, but he already knows where I live. My plan is to ask him to my flat so I can make pizza. I haven't talked it over with Yenta yet, but it could work, couldn't it?

Okay, I need to stop and act before I overthink the whole thing.

I get out my phone, in the middle of the wood as Bessie runs back and forth across the path in search of whatever scent she can pick up. She's happy for a little bit while I stay in one place to use the phone.

You should never walk and talk on the phone, it's dangerous. Driving and talking on the phone is dangerous too. I always get funny looks for pointing this out, but people need to know how dangerous it is. I'm doing them a favour. They shouldn't be so bloody annoyed about it. They should thank me for trying to help.

I saved Stephan's number as soon as he gave it to me. I don't know his last name, though, and when you save a phone number there's a space for a last name. I don't like to leave blanks, so I put his last name as 'Spring'. I find that funny, since my last name is Winters and if his was really Spring, we would kind of go together. We did meet in the snow, he was a bit of warm sunshine on that icy cold, embarrassing day. I suppose he'd rather forget the entire incident. I would too, except I'd have to forget the first time I saw his beautiful, spring morning eyes.

Oh, well. I sort out in my head what I'm going to say. I quickly jotted down some notes before I came out. I hold my phone in one hand and the notes in the other, including a list of possible replies he might make. Here goes. I press connect.

"Er, hello?" he answers on the first ring.

"Hello, Stephan? This is Kit Winters. I don't know if you remember—"

"Oh god, yes, yes, I remember." He sounds out of breath. "How could I forget? Kit, hello."

"Erm, oh, Hello. Stephan. You said I should think about where I'd like to go and eat, and I've thought about it. I hope I haven't taken too long. I mean, I hope you haven't decided to do something else instead… What I'm saying is, yes, I'd like to go on a date with you… Hello?"

There's a sort of crashing sound and a shout. I wonder what I've interrupted. I listen for a moment. Is he still there? I'm about to ask when he speaks again.

"Look, Kit." His voice sounds a bit high-pitched and crackly. "I'm really sorry, but something's come up. This isn't really a good time."

I'm not very good at understanding different tones of voice, but he still sounds out of breath and now a bit stressed. There's some background noise, water by the sounds of it. Oh dear. Have I called him while he was taking a bath, or walking somewhere, or worse, driving?

"Oh, no, I'm sorry, Stephan. I should call back. When would be a good time?" I should have asked that at the beginning and then he could have told me straight away. I feel bad now. Everything is going wrong. I knew I should have texted. Oh god.

"Don't apologise, Kit. You couldn't know. I'm sorry, after you've taken all this time to... Anyway, could you call me back in like twenty minutes, do you think? I do want to talk to you. Please? I'm really sorry—ah—that I can't talk right—ouch—now."

"Are you all right?" I ask, because now it sounds like he's in pain.

"No, no, sorry, yes, yes, I'm—fucking hell, that's bloody cold—yes, I'm fine. Don't worry. I'll speak to you in about twenty minutes, Kit, I promise."

"O-okay." The call disconnects and I frown at my phone, as if it might give me some answers. I know I could ask the phone, but whilst Siri sometimes knows the answers to my questions, she most likely won't know what is wrong with Stephan and why he couldn't talk right now.

Well, that was confusing and a bit of a disaster. There are so many things I could have done better. The call only lasted forty-five seconds. This is why I don't do friends and relationships or even casual acquaintances when a forty-five-second conversation on the phone ends up a confusing mess. Still, he wants me to call him back. Maybe the second time will be a bit more organised.

Now I have a little time to think about everything that was said. Why did he sound like he was in pain? Was he in pain? What was it he said about something being cold? It's all very puzzling.

"Bessie?" I call, because whilst I was on the phone she's disappeared up the track. She doesn't usually stray too far from my side, unless there's exciting new snow to drive her batty, or she's found a really interesting smell.

Oh dear, I hope she doesn't roll in it, whatever it is she's found.

I can hear her barking, so she hasn't gone that far.

"Bessie?"

She barks in response but doesn't appear on the track. Where the hell is she? I haven't got a plan in place for if she runs off again. I was just hoping she wouldn't do it after that first time. Why won't she come?

"Bessie?" I call, feeling a little more panicked as I shine my head torch about, trying to see where she might be hiding. I clench my fists, digging my nails into my palms. I have gloves on, though, so I can't feel it. "B-Bessie?"

"She's here." A voice calls out at the same time as Bessie begins to bark continuously.

There's too much noise. I can't process it. Someone is shouting and Bessie is barking. I put my hands over my ears and freeze. Bessie needs to stop, but I can't see her and she's too far away. I can't shout because that would just add to the noise.

"Kit?" the voice calls again, and I hear it clearly above Bessie's barking because it's my name, and I suddenly realise I recognise the owner of the voice.

"Stephan?" I shout out. "Where are you?"

"Yes, through here, in the trees at the side of the track. Bessie, go and find Kit. Find Kit, girl. Good girl."

Bessie appears, bounding towards me from further up the track, and my limbs are suddenly free of their paralysis.

"Oh, thank god," I greet her as she jumps up at me. I don't even tell her off because I'm so relieved to see her. Then I remember what else is going on. "Where's Stephan, Bessie? Take me to Stephan."

I'm not really sure if she understands me, but her retriever instinct, crossed with her beagle sense of smell, seems to comprehend what I want her to do. She takes off down the track, stopping a few paces ahead to make sure I'm following before running off again, with me in careful pursuit because the track is really quite icy and slippery.

Around a bend in the track, I stop. Before me is a sight I just didn't expect, so it takes me a little while to make sense of it.

Alongside this part of the track there is a drainage ditch. It is usually filled with water, or varying degrees of mud. Today, it is filled with a combination of icy water, slush, mud…and Stephan.

"Stephan?" I exclaim.

"Hello, Kit." He smiles, but it doesn't have his usual spring morning brilliance.

"What are you, er, doing here?"

"I'm sitting in a frozen, slushy pool," he tells me, as if this is something I haven't already worked out.

"Er, why?"

"For the fun of it, Kit," he snaps, sounding a bit angry as he splashes the water around him with the palms of his hands.

"Oh, I see." I frown. What he said doesn't match the expression on his face. "You don't look like you're having fun."

He heaves a deep sigh and pinches the bridge of his nose, grimacing as water drips down from his fingers and over his lips and chin. "That's because I'm not. I was being sarcastic, I'm sorry." He says all this through gritted teeth.

"Oh, I see." I'm still a bit confused. "How did you get there?"

"I fell, Kit. I was running, and I slipped and fell."

"Oh no, are you hurt? Do you need help? I know first aid. I did a course at the library last year. It lasted six weeks, one hour a week, on Tuesdays." I stop when his expression changes from annoyed to something else I can't interpret. "I'm sorry, you probably didn't need to know that. Do you want me to help you out of that ditch?"

"Yes, please." Stephan is smiling again. I think he's relieved I've stopped talking.

I get as close to the edge of the ditch as possible and extend my hand for him to grab hold of. Bessie is trying to help too, but she thinks it's a game. I don't need to write down any plan for this, because it's pretty easy to predict what could happen. Stephan is taller than me, so probably heavier. Bessie is not really helping, as she jumps into the ditch and starts splashing about, trying to lick

Stephan's face, or any part of him she can get to. With a startled cry, I end up in the ditch with Stephan, sitting on his lap, in fact.

I gasp as the icy water seeps through my layers of clothes. For a moment, time stands still as Stephan's arms wrap firmly around me and hold me in position to stop me struggling.

"Steady on. You're all right. I've got you," he says in a soothing tone much like the one Yenta uses to help me calm down.

It does the job and I stop thrashing about and sit still in his lap. The water is cold, but I somehow don't notice it so much as I do the warmth of his arms around me and the look on his face as I fix my gaze on the spring light sparkling in his eyes.

"That's the second time you've ended up in my lap, Kit. We have to stop meeting like this." He smiles.

"Huh." I try to smile in response to his smile, but my teeth are chattering with the cold. "I have to stand up."

I wish I could have said something different. Something a little more appropriate. I recognise the way he spoke, because it sounded like a line from a movie, when the two main characters are flirting. I want to be able to flirt back, but I can never think of anything to say in the time allowed. Now it's too late, because he's already pushing me off his lap and letting me pull myself to my feet using the long, thick marsh grass that grows along this side of the track.

Once I'm up, I turn and extend my hand to him again. "Second try," I say, trying to smile and make it sound light-hearted. The truth is I'm worried that the same thing will happen again if I don't call Bessie to heel, but if I stop to do that, then Stephan will be left longer in that pool of freezing water, and I can't help noticing that he's wearing a lot less than I am. He's in danger of getting hypothermia. I know that because of the first-aid course I did.

There are too many thoughts in my head now. I need to organise them into a list. My hands cover my ears as I try to sort it all into a workable order, then I click my fingers as I mutter to myself.

"Bessie first, then Stephan, then think about first aid." Finally having everything sorted in the order I need to do it, I say, "Bessie. Heel." I keep my tone firm. She does as she is told. I can now concentrate on Stephan. "Sorry. I'll help you up now. Did you say if you were hurt?"

"I can't tell, I'm so bloody frozen," he replies through teeth that are chattering more than mine.

"Oh dear." I grab his hand and pull.

He scrambles up the side of the ditch with my help and ends up on the track, on his knees, breathing hard and looking rather pale. Muddy water drips off his hair and down his arms. I look him over and see he has lost a shoe. He's wearing running gear. Something is connecting in my brain. Was he running when I phoned him? Was that why he sounded out of breath? Did he fall when he was speaking to me?

"Oh god, was this my fault?" I ask him in shock. "Did you fall because I phoned you?"

He looks up at me, his expression one of surprise.

"No!" He gasps. "How could this have been your fault? It was my own stupid fault for answering the phone. I shouldn't have, but I've been, you know, waiting for this important phone call for days now."

I grimace. "And instead you got me. Oh god, Stephan, I'm sorry."

His expression has changed again. Good lord, I can't keep up with all the emotions he's feeling. He looks like he wants to say something, then thinks better of it. Instead, he heaves another sigh, then holds out his hand.

"Help me up, will you?"

I pull him to his feet, and he takes a step then immediately collapses to the ground with a loud cry. I understand the expression on his face now as he grabs his right ankle and begins to massage it. He's in agony.

"You *are* hurt." I fall to my knees beside him but don't touch him in case he doesn't want me to.

"Yes, I must have twisted my bloody ankle." He hisses through his teeth. "I'll need some help to get home, Kit. Will you help me?"

"Of course I will, although—" Oh dear. Now I'm in a pickle. "I don't have a plan for this. "I was going to make a plan for getting to your house once I'd asked where you live, but I haven't asked yet, and I haven't asked if it's okay for Bessie to come along as well, since she's here and I can't leave her. So, yes, I'll help you, but I don't know where you live."

Stephan smiles, and snorts a small laugh through his nose, his eyes twinkling, reflecting the sparkle of my torchlight. "Oh my god, you are so…" He chuckles. "That's okay, lovely boy. I know where I live. I'll tell you. You can even put it into Google maps so you can see where it is."

"Oh, that's okay. That's okay. Thank you." I smile and nod as I get out my phone. "But I'm not a boy, just so you know. I'm twenty-four."

I'm just opening the map app when he makes another noise that sounds like frustration. I put my phone away quickly, but he stops me with a hand on my wrist.

"It's okay, I'm not angry with you. I just realised, I dropped my phone in that stupid ditch."

"Oh, that's okay. Bessie will find it. That's what she's trained to do. Bessie." I call her over from the position I made her stay just a few minutes before. "Find Stephan's phone." I tell her. "His phone, Bessie. Find the phone."

Bessie regards me with her head tipped to one side and her tongue lolling out, in her 'thinking pose', before jumping feet first into the icy, muddy ditch. There's a fair bit of scrabbling about, whining, grunting and yelping and Stephan laughs out loud as he shuffles to get a better view. After about a minute of searching Bessie jumps back out of the ditch with something in her mouth. She shakes herself dry, showering both of us in great globs of freezing mud and slush before dropping Stephan's shoe at my feet. She immediately turns, jumps back into the ditch and repeats the process, this time dropping the retrieved phone at my feet and sitting back waiting for her reward.

"Bloody hell," Stephan exclaims and I can't help smiling. "She's found it. That's my phone and my shoe. She's a beaut. What a star, owned by a star."

I never know how to respond to praise without sounding either bad-tempered or awkward. Instead I make a fuss of my lovely dog, because she is the true star, even though she is covered in mud and worse. I fish in my pocket for a treat, give it to her, and then hand Stephan his phone and shoe.

"I'm afraid your phone is a bit wet and probably knackered," I say with a note of regret and sympathy.

He shrugs. "I can put it in rice when I get home. Heard that does the trick. And if it doesn't…shit happens, I suppose." He shrugs again and puts the phone in a holder he's wearing around his arm. "Now, how about getting me home, because I'm bloody freezing. Important parts of my anatomy are going to start falling off if I don't get warm soon."

"Oh no!" I gasp. "Here, you can have my coat." I unfasten it and hand it to him. "It's wet as well, but not quite so soaked as you are, since it's waterproof and kept some of the water out."

"I can't take your coat, then you'll be cold."

"No I won't. I've still got two jumpers on, a T-shirt and a vest. Yenta always says I should wear layers to keep warm when I'm walking Bessie in the winter. Although, technically this is now spring, but with winter weather. That's very confusing."

"It is, yes." Stephan is looking at me in a funny way, and it makes me feel a bit awkward. I don't really know what he's feeling now, but he accepts my coat, so that's okay. Now I don't need to worry about him getting cold. I just need to worry about how I'm going to help him home because he's quite a bit taller than me and I'm not very strong.

Turns out he doesn't live far. At the hotel, in fact.

"You live in the hotel?" I ask in surprise after he tells me. "Like, where you work? Just like me, living above Yenta's shop."

"Yes. That's something we have in common." His voice sounds strained, and he's gritting his teeth, probably because he's in pain. I wish I could take it away, or somehow take it into myself. I always feel so helpless in situations like this. That's why I did that first-aid course. But it still can't help him when he's in pain. I hate to think he's in this situation because I picked that precise moment to phone him. Especially when he was waiting for another phone call, which he won't get now because his phone is waterlogged.

"I'm sorry you won't get your important phone call now, Stephan. Did the person have your landline? Maybe they'll call you on that."

"That's okay, Kit. I already got the phone call I was waiting for."

I give him a puzzled look. "You said you answered the phone because you were waiting for an important call but instead you got me."

"No, not instead. Yours was the call I was waiting for, Kit."

"Oh. I—er—okay." I can't think why my call would be so important, since it was just to ask him if it was okay if we either went to eat at Subway or ate pizza at my flat for our date. Of course, he doesn't know this, because he fell into the ditch before I got the chance to ask him. "Why didn't you tell me you'd fallen into a ditch? I would have come to help. I wasn't far away."

"Yeah, but I didn't know that at the time, Kit, and it was kind of embarrassing."

"No more embarrassing than the things I've done. You caught me googling you in the library."

"Ooer, it's terrible when someone googles you in the library."
He giggles.

"Yes, I know, and I already apologised for that, but I didn't know your name."

"I was joking, Kit, and I know you apologised. Now you know my name, and I know yours." He grunts as we stumble over a bump in the track. "Jesus, that hurt. Could you g-give me a minute?"

He looks very pale, and I'm afraid he might pass out. Fortunately, I remember how to help because of that first-aid course.

"If you pass out, I know what to do," I reassure him. "I know what to do if you suffer a heart attack, a fit, bleeding, vomiting, lacerations, fainting, going into medical shock, migraine, nosebleed—"

"Kit, I get the idea, but I've just hurt my ankle, mate. I don't think I'm going to die."

"I don't think you are either. At least I hope you're not. I don't even know your last name yet. I can't keep calling you Mr. Spring."

"Mr. what?" He gapes at me. Oh god, he thinks I'm a freak. "My last name is Cassillis," he adds, thankfully not asking about the Spring thing.

"Oh good. I can put that in my phone now. Stephan Cassillis. It sounds nice."

"Not as nice as Kit Winters. And I like that you called me Spring. Winter and Spring go together quite nicely."

"I was just thinking that, yes, they do, if one lets the other in. This spring has been full of winters."

"Yes, and I wish this Spring was full of Winters too." Stephan mutters beneath his breath, words I don't think I'm supposed to have heard. He coughs, clearing his throat and smiling as if to hide the fact he's said something wrong. "I'm good to go now," he says, still smiling. "And while we're walking, why don't you tell me all about that first-aid course?"

"Really?" I ask, wondering if he's serious. "Because I can, but you know, if you're being funny, or sarcastic, I can't always tell."

"I'm not being sarcastic. Talk to me, Kit. You could read me the Shipping Forecast and I'd be mesmerised. You've got the loveliest voice, and I want to know everything about you."

So, with Bessie bounding around our feet like she's trying to herd us and me trying very hard to make sure Stephan doesn't put much weight on his injured ankle, we make our way to Stephan's hotel and I tell him all about first aid.

Chapter Five

Bessie Is Almost a YouTube Sensation
or
I Don't like Wearing Other People's Clothes

A ND THAT DOESN'T actually work, you know. Rice doesn't absorb the water fast enough for it not to do any damage. What you need is a desiccant. I've got some in my flat. I collect all those little packets you get in shoe boxes because I once dropped my phone down the toilet and had to get a new one, and it took me ages to decide what to get because they'd stopped making the model I dropped. Now I know how to dry it out properly so I don't have to go through all the rigmarole of finding a new phone."

Stephan is still listening avidly to everything I say as we finally hobble into the foyer of his hotel. I'd finished talking about first aid, and when he told me to talk about something else, anything, I started talking about drying phones out, because that seemed relevant.

"Steph." A voice startles me into silence, as a large, tall man, with grey eyes and wearing a smart suit strides quickly across the foyer to join us. "What happened, son?"

"Dad, I'm okay. I fell when I was out running. Kit rescued me. This is Kit." He smiles as he waves his free hand at me. I'm still standing with Stephan's other arm over my shoulder.

The man regards me with narrowed eyes. "Oh, so you're Kit," he says in an ominous way that makes me want to hide, and my hands are full of Stephan, so I can't shake this man's hand, not that he offers his to shake, but that means I can't say hello properly. He's turned away before I can do anything about it.

"It's okay," Stephan whispers in my ear, the sensation sending shivers down my spine that aren't unpleasant. "You can say hello properly when he's heard what happened to me. He won't mind that it's all in the wrong order. He's my dad, by the way. George. George Cassillis."

I nod, feeling a little disconcerted that he knew to even say that to me. How did he know? Is he psychic? I mean, I know that's not a real thing, but Stephan seems to have some sort of magic all of his own. It's almost as if he has a contingency plan just for dealing with me and all my quirks before he even knows what any of those quirks are.

"Right, Kit, take him into the lounge, while I get him some decent clothes to wear." He looks Stephan up and down and snorts. "What the hell are you wearing anyway? Running shorts? Steph, you've never gone running in your life."

Stephan looks a little embarrassed as I help him towards the large, well-lit room his dad has indicated.

"Oh god, Dad. There's a first time for everything, y'know. And Kit got a bit wet as well. He might need a change of clothes."

"Oh, no, thank you. I'm not… I mean, I don't want to seem ungrateful, and thank you for the offer, but I don't like…" I grimace. How can I tell Stephan that I don't like to wear other people's clothes without seeming like a bit of a snob?

"That's okay, lovely boy. I understand," Stephan whispers, saving me the job of explaining. What does he understand, though? I didn't explain anything. "Bessie here will probably need a rub down with a towel or something," Stephan continues, pointing at my very wet, muddy dog.

"Good god, it's the bloody Beast of Bodmin that crashed the wedding the other night," Stephan's dad exclaims.

I grimace, waiting for the inevitable fallout that I have managed to avoid for an entire week now. I prepare to deliver the apology of the century, but am surprised to find that Stephan and his dad are laughing.

"Oh my god, Kit." Stephan's dad directs his smile at me. "I have watched the footage of your dog having a blast at that wedding party on CCTV so many times in the last week. If I could, I'd upload it to YouTube. It would go viral for sure. The wedding party was a bit of a disaster from beginning to end, however, ending in a massive bust-up in the car park."

"Yes, Stephan told me." I glance at Stephan for reassurance and he nods encouragement.

He's settled in a comfy sofa now, with a footstool to elevate his injured ankle.

"Right." Stephan's dad chuckles. "I'll be with you in a sec with a towel and some clean clothes for the wounded soldier, and then we can decide whether he needs an amputation, or just a stiff drink."

I try to make sense of what he's saying as I take a seat next to Stephan, trying to keep Bessie from making a mess of anywhere by jumping up onto the sofa with us.

"There aren't any soldiers here, Stephan," I whisper as Stephan's dad disappears from the room. I know what he really means, of course, but things like this, they play over and over in my mind when I'm a little stressed and I have to talk them out or they drive me crazy. "And he's not really going to cut your foot off, is he? I mean, I'm not a doctor, but I think it's only sprained. And even if it was broken, that doesn't warrant an amputation, not in the twenty-first century, anyway. Maybe if we were living in the eighteen hundreds, as pirates, then you'd probably end up with a wooden leg. That would be pretty cool. I mean, to be a pirate, obviously, not to lose your leg."

"Oh, god, Kit, you're so bloody adorable, I could eat you in a sandwich," Stephan says in response to my anxious mumblings, his forehead leaning very close to mine.

I lean back a little and give him a startled look. He smiles.

"Not literally, obviously," he clarifies. "I don't really want to make you into a sandwich and eat you, it's just a way of saying that I…" He doesn't finish the sentence because we are interrupted by another man entering the room.

"All right, sport?" He has a bit of an accent, a smirk on his face, and he's wearing a chef's hat and an apron. "What the fuck happened to you, then?" He looks Stephan up and down and snorts. "And what the hell are you wearing? Are they running shorts?"

"Yes, Guy, they are. What of it?" Stephan asks, sounding just a little unhappy. Maybe because it is the second time he's been asked this. Why would it be so surprising? People wear running shorts all the time.

Guy just snorts again in response but says nothing more about Stephan's clothes. Another person joins us, a woman, possibly my age. She bypasses me and goes straight to Stephan's side.

"Steph, what happened?"

"Lisa." Stephan smiles. "I fell. Kit here rescued me. Oh, and Bessie." He adds. At the sound of her name, Bessie jumps up to try and lick his face.

I grab her collar and draw her away. "Bessie, heel!" I gasp, shocked by her behaviour and worried that we'll be sent away if she doesn't behave. I'm not sure if dogs are even allowed in hotels. I'm sure Stephan's dad would have said something if that were the case, but I'm also sure that, considering Bessie's track record at this particular hotel, we'll be thrown out for sure if she does anything else outrageous.

Stephan laughs at her antics. "It's okay, Kit. She's just glad to be somewhere warm and dry." He turns back to the woman he called Lisa. "Lis, will you do me a favour and take my shoe off? Loosen the laces as much as you can, would you?"

The woman purses her lips and doesn't look very happy but does as she is asked whilst the other man, still laughing, sits beside Stephan in my place. It does feel like he's taken my place, but I suppose I did move and I don't really have any claim to sit closer to Stephan than anyone else.

I should have helped Stephan with his shoe, but I didn't think about it. Now he has someone else to help. I watch, trying not to stare because I know how uncomfortable people get when I do. The woman manages to get Stephan's trainer off, with poor Stephan looking very unhappy and pale. She's about to start with his sock when I step forward.

"No, leave the sock on," I say, rather too loudly, shocking her into turning to me and leaving go of Stephan's foot. He cries out as she drops it, and I grimace because that was partly my fault, but if she tries to take his sock off now... "You need to leave the sock on until some of the swelling has gone down. It'll be easier to get it off then, and it won't hurt as much." I risk meeting Stephan's gaze.

"Best listen to Kit there, Lisa. He knows his stuff." He smiles at me and winks.

Oh! That was a little unexpected. I'm never really sure what a wink means, but in this case I assume it means he's happy with what I've said. The woman, however, looks a little cross.

"Kit, this is Lisa, my sister."

I smile and hold out my hand. "Hello, Lisa, I'm Kit."

She stands, but doesn't take my hand, staring at it as if it's got spikes or something. "Er, yes. Stephan just said," she says through pursed lips.

Oh no. Somehow I've managed to mess this up. I know that look she's directing at me. I've seen it too many times before.

"Y-yes, of course he did. I-I'm sorry," I mumble as I take a step back.

"Lisa, I'd love a cuppa," Stephan interrupts before I can make the conversation any more awkward. "Do you think you could make me one, and something for Kit? He did rescue me after all." Stephan's request distracts his sister, and she directs her gaze at him instead of me.

"I'm not your slave," she snaps. "Get Guy to do it. He's quite happily sitting on his backside. You might have hurt yourself and I sympathise, but you're still an arse for going out jogging in the first place when you've never jogged in your entire life, and all in the hope you might meet some bloke you've been crushing on who hasn't even had the decency to call you back yet."

"Holy crap, Lisa," Stephan hisses at her, his head doing a funny twitch in my direction, his face stuck in some sort of tight grimace. "Could you have said that any louder? Open your mouth a bit more and you'll fit the other foot in as well."

"Oh god, is that him?" she whispers, turning her back on me so I can't see her expression. I might not be very good at picking up social cues but I'm pretty sure they're talking about me. I can't quite work out why, though.

Stephan answers his sister, but I don't listen. Yenta says it's wrong to eavesdrop, even when she does it all the time. Instead, I back away, until my heels hit a wall. I don't listen, but I do watch. Stephan hisses a few more words and Lisa leaves, directing an angry glare my way.

Half my problem is that I never know what I've done to make people angry. I must have done something to make her react that way, but I have no idea what. I am well out of my comfort zone here: an unfamiliar place, with no contingency plan, and unfamiliar people whom I haven't had a chance to meet properly. The guy sitting next to Stephan keeps giving me weird looks. I should leave before I'm overwhelmed, but I don't want to until I'm sure Stephan is okay, and he doesn't look okay. He still looks pale, and I wish I could do something for him, but I can't, and that makes me feel even worse.

"Got some ice." Stephan's dad returns at that moment with a bag of ice and lays it on Stephan's foot as gently as he can. "Now, tell me how this happened, Steph? Were you really out running?"

Stephan starts to tell his story, and the two men draw closer to listen. Stephan's sister returns, but by that time, I'm too stressed to notice if she's staring at me or not. There are too many people in the room. Too many voices all at once. My brain can't process any of it. I'm going to lose it in front of Stephan and his entire family and there isn't a thing I can do about it.

I'm drowning in a sea of words, with no way of sorting it all out into some sort of order.

I can feel myself floating free and out of control. I clench my fists, digging my nails in as hard as I can to get the sensation of pain rather than feel the chaos threatening to overwhelm me.

Bessie pushes her nose against my hand and forces me to open it so I can pat her head. I feel calmer almost immediately.

When someone asks me what Bessie actually does, I'm never sure what to tell them because I can't adequately describe it. She isn't there to find stuff, or warn me, or guide me, like other assistance dogs, although she has been trained to retrieve, but that's just in her nature. I don't need assistance. I can look after myself. What she does do is provide an anchor. Her job is to be with me without expecting anything from me in return, and that simple action of pushing her head into my hand calms me and grounds me like nothing else ever has.

I'm still in a very stressful situation, but she's there and she isn't leaving me, not even when someone offers her a bowl of water at Stephan's request. She'll be thirsty, but she won't leave my side until I'm ready.

"Kit?" Stephan's voice sounds distant, echoey, and usually nothing can get through the fog in my brain once it has taken hold. Somehow, his voice finds an opening. I force myself to look at him. He's alone now. Everyone else is gone. "Okay?" He looks concerned, but not in a bad way.

"Yes." I nod. "I just needed some, erm, space, I'm sorry."

"No need to apologise, mate. Take all the time you need."

"Maybe I should go." I still feel wobbly, on edge, but it's not as bad as I thought it was going to be. I still might flip, though, and I can't let Stephan see me like that.

"Only when you're ready," Stephan says. "I sent everyone else away. It's just you and me, and I'll shut up until you're ready to talk."

I nod, swallowing hard and feeling my mouth getting very dry which reminds me that Bessie needs a drink of water. "Drink, Bessie. It's okay now."

She goes to the bowl that was set out for her and drinks noisily. I focus on that sound and take some deep breaths to push the last of the panic away. When I'm sure it's all gone, I look up and find Stephan's eyes watching me, a soft smile on his lips. He waits.

"How do you know?" I ask him, frowning.

He tips his head to one side. "Know what?"

"What to do. That I need you to wait? Did Yenta tell you?"

"No." He shakes his head. "I just felt like that was the right thing to do."

"And you sent everyone else away because of me. Were they angry?"

"Not because of you. They were doing my head in as well, mate. My family can be loud and they swear. A lot. It's embarrassing sometimes, the way they fuss. And you don't need to go repeating that to them either, because I know I should be grateful I've got such attentive relatives."

I find myself smiling. "I won't. I promise."

"I trust you." He smirks. "Come and sit over here, only if you want, obviously. If you need to go, then go. I can speak to you another time."

"Another time?"

"If you want, that is, since I assume you called me because you wanted to either make a date for dinner or tell me to go to hell."

"I would never tell you that." I feel horrified that he would think that. "Jesus, Stephan."

"I'm sorry." He lowers his gaze.

"How's your ankle?" I ask. It's easier for me to change the subject than to try and think of something to say in response to his apology. I walk over to take a look at his ankle now that I can.

"The swelling is still pretty bad. There's bruising too." I point at some rather alarming discolouration along the side of his foot.

"I know." He makes a face. "Dad wants to take me to A and E."

"Oh. Then I should probably go." I make a move towards the door, but he catches my hand, the touch so unexpected I jump.

"I'm sorry." He pulls his hand away quickly. "I didn't mean—I just wanted to make sure you didn't run away and disappear from my life completely, because I do want to see you again, Kit." He looks up at me. "At least consider that dinner date, please?"

"I don't like restaurants," I tell him.

He nods, and pats the sofa beside him, giving no indication that he thinks the way I just blurted out that fact is weird. I sit, straight-backed as I try to order my thoughts enough to tell him what I originally wanted to say on the phone.

"I'm a bit of a fussy eater, I mean, I'm not fussy in a fussy way. I don't like it when other smells interfere."

"Smells?"

"Yes, restaurants, they smell. Too many different dishes, everyone ordering different things, and it stops me from tasting what I'm eating because of all the other smells. Also, people get dressed up to go to restaurants. They wear perfume and aftershave, and my food ends up tasting of that as well."

"Where do you prefer to eat then?" he asks, watching me carefully.

I bite my lip. "You won't think I'm weird?"

"Why would I think that? What you've just said makes perfect sense to me."

"Oh. Well, I like Subway. All Subways smell the same, because everyone is ordering the same things. I mean, you can smell Subway from the other end of the high street, even before you see the sign."

"This is true." Stephan laughs in surprise as if he's only just realised this himself.

"Anyway, at Subway, you can order the exact same thing every time. The people there remember my order now, and they do it the same way. They even made a list to give to new members of staff."

"That was good of them."

"Yes." I nod. "I mean, If I'm just ordering for myself I don't even have to speak to anyone. They just get my order ready for me. Of course, sometimes I have to order for Yenta as well, and she orders something different each time. Actually, I'm convinced she does it to force me to, you know, be sociable." I grimace, because I know that everything I've just told him is making it clearer and clearer that I'm more than different, I'm pretty damn weird.

Quirky, my mum used to say to me. *"You're not weird, Kit, you're quirky. Just because you do and say and think a little differently to everyone else does not make you any less than them."*

"Kit, are you saying that you'd be happy if we went to eat at Subway?" Stephan asks.

Oh dear. I knew this was a mistake. Subway was never going to be an acceptable location for a first date. I should have told him about the pizza straight away.

Yenta always says I should have a plan B, and I did have something all worked out—in case Stephan hates Subway—but now, with everything else that's happened, I can't get it all sorted in my head. I need to read what I've written down, but doing that will just highlight more of my oddness.

Besides, I still don't know why he even wants to spend time with me. "Why?"

"Why what, mate?" He frowns. I know I have difficulty keeping up with what people are saying to me, but I also know that what I say can be pretty difficult to decipher as well.

"Why do you want to, you know, go on a date with me?"

"Why do you want to go on a date with me?" he counters.

"I asked you first."

He chuckles. "You did indeed." He twists his lips as he thinks. "Well, apart from the fact that I could just sit and listen to you talking all night, I think you're really kind of cute and I'd like to get to know you better. Much better."

"Oh, okay, well, same, really. I-I mean, I'd like to get to know you. I don't have many friends. I'm a bit too much all at once sometimes."

"I can't get enough of you, Kit." Stephan's confession takes me a bit by surprise, and I can't really think of anything to say in response. "Kit?" He speaks instead.

"Yes?" I'm staring down at my hands, and am slightly startled when his hand appears and covers both of mine.

His skin is warm and rough and firm against mine.

"You know these contingency plans you have?"

"Y-yes," I stutter, surprised that he's remembered about them at all.

"Do you have a contingency plan for when someone wants to kiss you?"

"I, er, wrote one a while ago, but I've never used it, because no one ever wants to kiss me. Not that I've tried going out and finding someone to kiss. I did once, but it was a bit of a disaster. The guy didn't want to do any kissing, he just wanted to…" I bite my lip to stop oversharing. "You probably don't want to know about that."

"Not right now, no," he agrees. "Maybe some other time, when I'm not trying to kiss you."

"Kiss me?" I squeak as I finally meet his spring-light gaze. "You want to kiss me?" It's all very intense, and I can see everything reflected in that sky blue.

"Yes, Kit, I do. May I?"

"Y-yes, because I really want to kiss you. I have since I first saw you."

"Oh, Kit, me too." He leans closer, and I hesitate, just a fraction of a second, but long enough for him to stop. "Okay?" he asks, waiting.

I take a little time to sort it all out, the kissing thing, in my head, and then I nod.

"Yes." And I press my lips to his.

They're drier than I expected, and warm, and soft, and they move against mine so gently I can barely feel them. That's no good, because I want to feel him kissing me.

I reach up and lace my fingers through his hair, pulling him closer and opening my mouth just a little. I'm rewarded with a feathery touch of his tongue against my bottom lip.

With a soft moan, I press further, my tongue seeking his, tasting him and finding that I like the taste very much. It's different, but not bad. I guess he hasn't eaten recently as I can't taste any food. He doesn't wear strong aftershave, but I knew that about him already. All I can smell is some sort of mild-smelling shower gel, and sweat, because he was running, but it's not overpowering. I can also smell mud and grass and snow. I quite like the smell of snow.

Correction: I quite like the smell of snow on Stephan.

I never know when kisses are supposed to end, and this one ends a bit awkwardly, with me pulling away while he's still trying to lick my bottom lip.

"S-sorry." I watch as he slowly opens his eyes and smiles at me.

"What are you sorry for?" he asks, drawing a finger down my cheek and making my entire face tingle in a good way. I catch my breath and return his smile.

"I-I don't know, I just thought that was a bit…"

"Awesome," he finishes the sentence for me, and everything about the way he said the word, and the way he's looking at me, and the way he's touching me, is just that. Awesome, and I've got this warm feeling in my stomach, and in other places too, that I haven't felt for such a long time, because I haven't met anyone that I've wanted to feel that way with, until now.

Oh, I know if I tell him all of this right now, I'll probably send him running for his life, even with a sprained ankle, so I keep my mouth shut. I'll get the chance to tell him eventually, I hope. Right now though, I think I need to go.

Out of the corner of my eye I can see Stephan's dad hovering in the doorway, and it's pretty obvious, even to me, that he's waiting to take Stephan to the hospital to get his ankle looked at.

"I have to go." I start to gather my stuff: backpack, coat, Bessie's lead. Stephan catches my hand in his and pulls it to his lips to kiss the back of it.

"Thank you," he whispers.

"What for?" I ask with wide eyes.

"For everything. For rescuing me. For being so bloody adorable, even though you don't know that you are, but that just makes you even more so."

"Bollocks." I chuckle. "I think those painkillers your dad gave you are starting to kick in."

He grins. "Maybe, maybe not." He looks up at me as I stand, releasing my hand as I do. "Should I call you to let you know how my ankle is?"

"Yes, er, could you text me instead, please?"

"Of course." He nods. "But how will I get to hear your voice again if I can only text you?"

"I could come and visit tomorrow," I suggest, not finding it at all difficult to think of this contingency plan. "I know the way here now, but is it okay if Bessie comes too? I don't know why, but she does seem to get a bit over-excited around you."

"I know the feeling." Stephan tells me, his smile broadening. "Of course she can come. I'll see you tomorrow then, Kit."

"Okay." I nod and then turn to leave, clicking my fingers to get Bessie's attention. She follows obediently.

At the door, I stop and look back. Stephan is watching me, that smile still on his face. I put that smile there. Me. I find that quite incredible, that such an awkward kiss could have such a positive effect. Anyway, I might get a chance to try that again tomorrow, unless he decides it wasn't so awesome after all. At least if he doesn't want to do anything more, I think I'll have made a friend.

I pass Stephan's dad as I leave. He smiles and nods.

"Goodbye, Kit."

I'm a little fazed, because I haven't really said hello to him properly yet, but then I remember Stephan telling me that his dad won't mind if we do things the wrong way around, so I smile and nod back at him.

"Bye, Mr., erm, Stephan's dad."

He walks into the lounge and I can hear him talking to Stephan as I fasten Bessie's lead to her collar.

"He's a bit of an oddbod, isn't he, Steph?"

I freeze, my heart suddenly pounding in my ears and the air roaring as I gulp in shallow breaths. Is he talking about me? Describing me the way almost everyone in the world sees me.

"Dad, don't say that," Stephan corrects him, and I can suddenly breathe a little easier. "I think he's perfect."

I leave through the main door as quickly as I can so that no one can think I might have been eavesdropping.

All the way home, Stephan's words play over and over in my head—*I think he's perfect. I think he's perfect*—until I end up saying them out loud like a chant.

How can he think that? But then, I've never been able to fathom the way others think, or what they mean when they say things like that about me.

I'm not perfect, but if Stephan wants to think that, who am I to argue?

Chapter Six

Planning Dates
or
Water Does Not Taste the Same
from Other People's Taps

MORNING BREAK IN the bookshop is for catching up on news. Yenta likes to hear about the things I've been doing when not at work, so today, I tell her everything that happened with Stephan the night before. Well, almost everything. I leave out the bit about kissing because I'm still processing that.

"His ankle is only sprained," I explain. "He texted me last night and I replied with a smiley face emoji, followed by a sad-faced one just in case he thought I was smiling at his misfortune and not just the fact that his ankle isn't actually broken."

"You could have called and spoken to him, Lapushka," Yenta chides gently.

I purse my lips then blow out my cheeks. "Yenta, you know I don't understand the rules of talking on the phone. I mean, I don't want Stephan to think I'm stupid."

"He won't think that, he likes you."

"Yes, I know." I nod, thinking a little more about our kiss and smiling. "He wants me to visit him today. He said so in his text and asked me last night. I replied with a thumbs up emoji."

Yenta sighs and shakes her head. "You should take him some flowers," she suggests as we finish our tea and get back to work.

"Flowers?" I ask in disgust. "Yenta, you know how I feel about flowers. I mean they're technically dead as soon as you pick them.

And they stink, and the smell only gets worse as they sit there in the vase slowly decaying before your very eyes. Why anyone thought cutting the heads off living things and presenting them as a—"

"Most people think it's romantic, Kit," She stops me in mid-rant. "And it's a traditional gift when visiting someone who is ill."

"But Stephan isn't ill. It's not as if he's going to die or anything. He hurt his ankle."

"Or when they're injured," she adds. I can see her rolling her eyes. She isn't going to convince me. "Chocolates, then." She suggests as an alternative.

"Chocolates would be better." I give the matter some thought. "But which brand? I can't just give him any old chocolates and hope he likes them. Maybe I should ask him." I get out my phone, glad of an excuse to send him a text that is more than a simple picture expressing emotion.

"Kit, you can't ask him what he likes, that would spoil the surprise," Yenta exclaims with a degree of frustration in her tone that even I can hear.

I put away my phone with a sigh. "Okay, but I still need to think about what brand he would like."

"Go to the chocolatier's along the high street and pick out some special ones."

"But Yenta, it's Wednesday!" I gasp. "You know I don't go shopping on a Wednesday."

"Not even for a special occasion?"

I scowl. She's right of course, but I hate to change my routine. Oh, I know I'm older now and have developed strategies to cope when my routine changes, but that doesn't stop me resisting any unnecessary deviations.

"Perhaps I could make him a cake," I suggest, mostly to myself, but Yenta hears and shakes her head.

"He lives in a hotel, Kit. He probably has cakes coming out of his ears."

"Out of his ears?" I repeat, and then it dawns on me that she doesn't literally mean the cakes are coming out of his ears. Still, the mental image the phrase conjures up makes me smile.

"What are you smiling at?" Yenta asks, smiling in return.

I smirk. "Just a mental image of Stephan."

"Oh, I probably don't even want to know, then." Yenta raises her eyebrows and returns her attention to her clipboard. I feel myself blushing.

"Oh no, nothing rude, Yenta. I promise."

"And why not?" she asks, her eyes twinkling and her eyebrows flicking up and down. "He's a good-looking boy."

"Yenta!" I exclaim in shock, laughing when she grins like a wicked witch. "He's hardly a boy, and neither am I, for that matter." I frown, thinking about the kiss we shared the night before.

I stare down at my feet, my cheeks burning. I've never felt comfortable discussing these things with anyone, but for some reason, Yenta seems a lot more accepting than anyone else I have ever met. Even my mum had difficulty understanding my attraction to men and not women. She never understood why I didn't want to follow the rules when it came to relationships and I never understood why she thought her set of rules were the only ones to follow.

And Yenta's take on the whole relationship thing?

"We make our own rules, Lapushka."

Of course, this makes no sense to me at all, because, if we all make our own rules, how am I supposed to know if my rules are compatible with someone else's? It's all very confusing, and then there's Stephan, who asked my permission before he kissed me. No one has done that before.

Apparently, Stephan has a set of rules that are completely unique, and I'm intrigued to say the least.

"He asked to kiss me, Yenta," I confess, still staring at my feet.

"Oh, did he indeed?" She leans a little closer. "And did you allow it?"

"Yes." My cheeks are flaming now.

"And, it was good, yes?"

"Yes, but that's not the point. I mean, it is the point, because the point was the kiss, that's why he asked, but it was the way he asked, like he understood. Just like everything else he does, it's like he understands me. I don't know how he can. We've only met five times. I know I said I wanted to write a manual about me, but it's as if he's already read it."

"I told you, it was obvious to me that he likes you a lot." She nods, pushing her glasses up her nose and stretching out her back muscles after being stooped over the box of books for too long. "When someone feels that way, they are willing to make an effort to learn all they can about the object of their affections."

"Affections?" I gasp. "But how can I be the object of his affections after such a short time?"

"Perhaps it is even love at first sight." She has a far-off look in her eyes, one that I recognise because she has it when she's discussing romance with some of her bookshop friends. I snort.

"Huh, don't be silly. That sort of thing only happens in stories and movies. Not in real life."

"It happened for me, Lapushka, when I met my Samuel. We knew the very first time we met."

"Knew what?" I ask, stepping down from the stool I was using to reach the top shelf.

I want to focus fully on what she's saying. When she talks about her husband, she always has such a gleam in her eyes, and when she should be sad because Samuel is dead and has been for fifteen years, she always seems so happy. The memories are still so vivid for her. It makes me wonder if I could ever have something like that with someone special. Should I even allow myself to hope that Stephan might be that someone special?

"I knew I would spend the rest of my life with that man." Yenta sighs with a dreamy look before shrugging and picking up her clip board again. "Oh, well, he got to spend the rest of his life with me, at least."

"I thought I'd found that with Harry, but he wanted something different." I feel the familiar panic whenever I think of my ex-boyfriend. "I didn't know until he left. He never told me. Left it for me to guess and I just can't guess things like that, but he didn't understand that. He thought I was just being deliberately stupid. And now I've met Stephan, I wonder if what I felt for Harry was anything like love at all. Not that I'm saying I love Stephan. I don't really know him, but everything feels different with him. I now understand what people mean when they say they have butterflies in their stomach. It does feel like there's something fluttering around in there."

Yenta steps up to me and smooths down the front of my T-shirt before flicking away a piece of fluff from my sleeve. "Love is different for everyone, Lapushka, and different every time."

That doesn't help me at all!

"So how am I supposed to know, if it's always different? How can I make any kind of contingency plan for that? It would take up reams and reams of note paper and probably take a lifetime to write."

"You understand more than you think you do, sometimes, Lapushka. Give yourself some credit." She reaches up and plants a kiss on my cheek. "And contingency plans aren't always appropriate. Sometimes you have to just go with the flow. In fact…" She smiles, tipping her head to one side. "Why don't you make that your contingency plan?"

"What? Going with the flow?" I gape at her. "I mean, I understand what you're trying to say, but there are far too many variables to just go with the flow, Yenta. Far too many."

Although, with Stephan, there's only him, and no one else. I suppose I could just listen to what the rest of my senses are telling me instead of planning it all in advance. He does seem very patient. I suppose I could do that with the chocolates as well, but this is assuming that whoever is serving in the chocolate shop today is going to be equally as patient.

"Yenta, I might just have a plan that isn't really a plan."

"Now that doesn't make any sense at all, whilst it makes every sense in the world. Tell me."

I frown as I try to sort out the order I will be doing things. "I'm going to go to the chocolate shop and ask the person behind the counter to choose the chocolates. That way, they won't ask me a million and one questions that I won't be able to answer. And then I'm going to take them to Stephan, sit beside him and wait to see what happens next."

"No contingency plans for making conversation?"

"Nope." I smile. "He always seems to have so much to say I probably won't need to speak, and when I do, he listens. He told me I could read the Shipping Forecast and he'd be mesmerised."

Yenta laughs. "You're not actually going to do that, are you?"

"Well, no, I hadn't planned on doing it." I regard her with one eye closed. "Do you think I should?"

"No! Goodness me, no." She grasps my shoulders and turns me towards the door. "Now go and get those chocolates for this man of yours, and while you're out there, get us some sandwiches for lunch. You have a contingency plan for that, don't you?"

"Yes, Yenta." I tell her automatically, but I'm smiling as I leave the shop.

***

After the bookshop closes I walk over to Stephan's hotel. Well, I know it isn't technically his, but it is where he works and lives so, it is his in a way. I bring Bessie, because I'm always better when she is nearby, especially when I'm going into new situations. I just hope yesterday wasn't a one-off and she'll still be welcome.

I haven't made a plan. In the foyer of the hotel, I realise my mistake. Until Bessiegate, I'd never been inside a hotel. I have no idea how this works.

Do I walk up to the reception and ask for him? He isn't staying here, he lives here. Does that mean there is a different set of rules? I could phone him to tell him I'm here, but he can't come out and meet me because he can't walk. What do I do now?

Bessie whines softly by my side, doing her best to calm me down, whilst I am stuck in an indecision feedback loop, fully aware that I am rocking backwards and forwards from my heels to my toes and trying not to wring my hands. A voice startles me.

"Kit?"

I whirl around to see Stephan's dad standing behind me. I look quickly at his face to check it is him, and then I look away. I'm already beginning to feel stressed. Looking will overwhelm me with information I don't really need. I'm pretty sure what his expression will be anyway. It will be the same as Stephan's sister's yesterday, when she just kept frowning at me as if I was some sort of alien.

"Hello, Mr., erm…" I am very bad at remembering names. I have forgotten his. "Mr., erm, Stephan's dad." I smile, glancing quickly at his face again. The smile seems to do the trick, because he smiles back, and if there was any sort of confused look on his face, it is gone now.

"You can call me George," Stephan's dad tells me. "I really don't mind." He crouches down to make a fuss of Bessie. "And you brought Bessie with you. Hello, girl."

"George, of course," I exclaim, clicking my fingers whilst his attention is on my dog and not me. "I remember now. Hello, George. I'm Kit." I hold out my hand for him to shake. When he gives me a startled look I grimace and tuck my hand behind my back. "I'm sorry. I mean, you know that already, but we weren't introduced properly yesterday, and I like to do things like that properly, and Stephan said you wouldn't mind if we did it the wrong way around, plus, I'm really bad at remembering names unless I've done things the right way around. Sorry, that didn't make any sense at all."

"It made perfect sense, Kit. And I might add that you don't seem to have any trouble remembering Stephan's name," George muses as he leads me towards a doorway.

"Oh, well, Stephan is different." I hope he won't ask for an explanation because I haven't got one. Instead, I open my mouth, and complete and utter rubbish comes out of it. "Of course, I didn't know his name at first so I had to keep calling him Mr. Spring."

"Mr. what?" George stops to look at me.

I grimace again. Oh god, why did I tell him that?

"I mean, sorry, it was just a silly nickname I gave him until I knew his real name, and it kind of matched mine, you know: Spring, Winter. It just fits." I stop because I know I've said too much by the glassy look in George's eyes. I'm glad I didn't blurt out the real reason I called Stephan 'Spring'. That would have really made me sound odd.

George narrows his eyes and then shakes his head. He looks as if he is smiling and trying not to laugh.

"Come on, I'll take you to where Stephan has set up his throne room."

"Throne room? Does he think he's a king?"

"Ha, he wishes." George laughs. "No, but he's acting like one, ordering us all about and having us pander to his every whim because he has to stay off his feet for a few days. He's driving me batty, I can tell you. I'm glad you're finally here so I don't have to listen to his bellyaching for a few hours."

"Does he have a bellyache too?" I'm worried now that he might really be ill as well as broken.

"No." George gives me a sideways look, stretching the word out. "But he will if he keeps on stuffing himself with cakes. Guy made him a get-well-soon selection."

"Oh, I knew that would happen. I almost baked him a cake, but I decided not to because I knew he'd already have some."

"Yes, he does. So many they're coming out of his ears."

This is so close to the mental image Yenta conjured up earlier, I laugh out loud, a noise that startles George, making him jump, but then smile and laugh as well.

He stretches out a hand towards the nearest door and I think he wants me to walk through first. This door looks like an exit, rather than a door into another room, however. I hesitate.

"W-why are we going outside?" I ask in a sudden panic. Is this when he finally tells me that dogs aren't allowed in his hotel? I knew I should have asked. I knew I should have...

"It's okay, Kit." George steps forward and tries to meet my gaze. "Stephan told me I should explain and I forgot. I'm sorry. We have to go this way to get to the private family apartment at the back of the hotel. The only other way is through the kitchens, and Stephan says you don't like the smells."

"That's right. I don't." I follow George through the door feeling a little more relaxed, but I keep a tight hold of Bessie's lead just the same.

I'm completely astounded that Stephan even gave this any thought. Most people dismiss my sensitivity to smells because they just don't understand how it can affect me in such an adverse way. I told Stephan about this only yesterday and he's made a whole plan about the route I'd need to take to get to him without passing through my worst nightmare: a commercial kitchen.

I follow George through a garden area, around the back of the hotel and into a conservatory which is currently very pleasantly warm because the sun is finally shining after a week of adverse winter weather.

The place has a domestic feel, like it is lived in, as opposed to the hotel foyer, which felt very clinical and intimidating. The fact that Stephan is here also helps the feelings of comfort.

"Hello, Kit." He smiles at me from a large, comfy sofa, his spring-light eyes setting those pretend butterflies fluttering about in my stomach again.

What is the matter with me? I only saw him yesterday. I'm acting like I haven't seen him in weeks and even then, I don't usually get this worked up about meeting someone.

"Come and sit down, mate." Stephan indicates the space next to him on the sofa.

Bessie pulls free of my hold and bounds over to greet him. With a gasp, I grab her and pull her back, only just stopping her from jumping into Stephan's lap.

"I'm sorry. She's excited to see you," I apologise in confusion. "She isn't usually this badly behaved. I wouldn't have brought her if I'd known she would be all over you."

"That's okay." Stephan grins at me. "It must be my magnetic personality, and I know you're more relaxed when she's around. I would never have asked you to leave her behind."

"Oh, okay." I nod, not looking at him, still confused by Bessie's unusually flighty behaviour and by my reaction to being this close to Stephan again. I mean, we only kissed once, but I suddenly have the urge to jump into his lap as well, so I understand Bessie's eagerness.

I take a seat at the other end of the sofa, not too far away from where he said, but not so close as to be invading his personal space. I deposit my backpack beside me on the floor and then direct my gaze at my hands to check they aren't doing something odd, like wringing in my lap, or that my fingers aren't flicking and flexing.

"Hello, Stephan." I smile, but I know I've made a mess of this. "I mean, I probably should have said that straightaway, before I sat down."

"That's all right. You know I don't mind doing things in the wrong order."

"Yes, yes, I knew that, yes." When I eventually look up, he's smiling at me. So, okay, maybe I haven't messed up that badly—yet.

"There's a bowl of water for Bessie over there." He indicates a bowl on the floor in the corner of the conservatory.

"Thank you." I smile at him, then show Bessie, watching as she drinks the same way she does everything else: with enthusiasm.

"Would you like something to drink?" Stephan asks. "Tea, coffee? I don't know what you like."

"I-I, erm…" His question takes me by surprise. I can't process it quickly enough. "I don't drink…" Well, that sounds stupid, because everyone drinks. For want of a better way to explain, I pull out a water bottle from the side pocket of my backpack and show it to him. "I brought my own water."

"Oh, water from our taps not good enough, then?" George mutters from his position to the side of the sofa.

I jump, startled because I'd forgotten he was still there. Oh god, has he just watched all that awkwardness? What must he be thinking? I can't look. Instead, I fix my gaze on Stephan.

Stephan's eyes flicker to his dad, and they narrow. "Dad!" He jerks his head to one side. George rolls his eyes and huffs.

"I'll leave you to it, then," he says, sounding unhappy. "Seems I've had my marching orders. Nice meeting you, Kit. Enjoy your water."

"Er, I erm…" I stop, because he's gone before I can form a suitable reply.

I watch him disappear through the door and wince when it slams shut. I turn to face Stephan again.

"Was your dad angry with me for bringing my own water? I mean, I drink tea at home, and with Yenta, but anywhere else, I only drink water. I usually bring my own because water tastes different from other people's taps."

I wring my hands in my lap, waiting for him to laugh, or tell me that's a stupid thing to say, because water tastes the same wherever you are, it's just water. Unless you're me, of course. But he doesn't say anything, not until I look up at him.

"Don't worry about it, Kit. My dad's just a grumpy old sod."

"Some people say that about me," I admit. "I mean, not the old bit, because I'm not, old that is. Not that your dad is old either, because he's not. Yenta is eighty, and I still don't think of her as old, really. I'm rambling, sorry."

"Ramble away, mate. I love it. Anyway, You've got reasons to be grumpy." Stephan's eyes sparkle as he smiles. "My dad doesn't need an excuse. He frequently wakes up grumpy and stays that way all day."

"But I do that," I say, worrying now, that he might not know me as well as he seems to.

"Perhaps," Stephan agrees, as he shuffles closer to me on the sofa. "I think I could live with your sort of grumpy. At least it makes sense."

"To who?" I ask, puzzled. "Because it often doesn't even make sense to me."

Stephan chuckles and reaches out to touch my cheek. I lean back a little, out of reach, regarding his fingers before I look up at his eyes again. Instead of stopping him from touching me at all, I grab his hand and hold it. That way, at least the touch isn't so light and I have a bit more control over it.

"You don't like being touched?" Stephan asks, and not in an annoyed way because I've just prevented him from doing something he wanted to do. He sounds curious.

"It's not that. I do like being touched, but light touch—it hurts my skin. You probably think that's a stupid thing to say."

"I don't think that at all. I don't like being tickled," he confesses. "Everyone tells me I should like it, that it should make me laugh, but it just makes my skin crawl, and it's an invasion of my space, and I always want to go and take a long hot shower after someone's done it."

I gasp. "That's exactly how I feel! Except it hurts as well, really stings, like a cut, or as if someone's scratching my skin with razor sharp nails."

"Ouch." Stephan grimaces, looking sympathetic.

And that's it, I've run out of things to say because I came here without a list or a plan. If I open my mouth again, I'm afraid something else even more odd will come out of it. Everything I've said to this man so far has emphasised just how different I am, and I know he seems to be okay with it all, but there's a limit, and I've decided that three odd things is enough, so now I have nothing more to say.

Instead, I stare at my hands, clenched tightly in my lap.

"Kit, are you nervous?" Stephan asks me.

I take a deep breath, understanding why he might think that.

"I am a little, but not because I'm nervous of you or anything like that, because I'm not. I'm holding my hands like this because if I don't, I'm afraid they'll do something inappropriate."

Stephan snorts, and when I look at him, startled by his reaction, I see his eyes are sparkling and he's smirking. What did I say to make him react like that?

"Oh." I shake my head when I realise why he thinks my explanation was funny. "I don't mean that sort of inappropriate. I mean, you know, like clenching my fists, or flexing my fingers. I do that sort of thing without thinking. It's just that some people think it's a bit odd."

"You go ahead and do what you want, mate," Stephan urges me. "I won't think it's odd at all. And if it starts getting inappropriate, all the better."

I frown for a moment, processing what he's said, before laughing and meeting his gaze.

He laughs too. "I think that's the first time I've heard you laugh." He grins. "You always seem so serious."

"That's because I'm always concentrating on what I'm supposed to be doing next. It's a difficult job being me."

"I would have thought it harder to try and be something you're not, Kit. Personally, I wouldn't want you to be anything but yourself."

"Sometimes being myself can be difficult for other people."

"Sod other people," Stephan exclaims. "I think you're perfect just the way you are."

I look up at him, feeling the honesty of his statement as if it is a solid thing I can hold in my hand. I recall when I'd heard him say this same thing to his dad the night before and just how amazing it had made me feel. I want to say something to him, to make him feel the same, but I know nothing I say will ever sound as good.

Instead, I blurt out the first thing I think of. It's the first thing I always think of when I think of him.

"I think you have lovely eyes," I say, grimacing when those lovely eyes widen in surprise. "I mean, I don't usually notice anyone's eyes. There's people I've known for years and I couldn't tell you what colour eyes they have, but I noticed yours. They're like a clear blue sky on a spring morning."

"Oh." Stephan looks a little stunned, and I look away, embarrassed.

"I know that sounds daft, because how can your eyes be the sky? But that's how I felt when we first met, and when I didn't know your name I called you Mr. Spring." I chuckle nervously, staring back down at my hands. "Yeah, silly, isn't it?"

"No," Stephan breathes, his hands closing firmly over mine. "Not at all. I think…" His voice cracks, and he clears his throat, swallowing hard as if he's struggling to speak. "Kit, that's the most romantic thing anyone's ever said to me."

I snort. "Bollocks. I don't have a romantic bone in my body."

"I'm telling the truth." Stephan's grip tightens. "No one has ever said anything like that to me before."

"Oh, well, okay. So you don't think it's silly?" I ask, just to make sure.

"No. I think it's wonderful. I think you're wonderful, in fact, I think I need to kiss you."

"O-okay, you know, you don't have to ask my permission every time."

"No, but I love the look on your face when I do. Kiss me," he demands, so I do.

The kiss tastes of spaghetti Bolognese and not in a bad way, not like a shop-bought sauce. It's more like the homemade kind. He's obviously had some for lunch and living in a hotel it was probably homemade. I can taste fresh basil with an underlying hint of toothpaste, since he must have cleaned his teeth before I got here.

His fingers are laced with mine, and it feels nice. His hand is warm and firm and somehow safe. I don't understand how that can be. We don't know each other well enough to feel this secure.

"Stephan." I stare at our joined hands after the kiss has ended, because if I look at his face, I will forget what I want to say, or get it all muddled up and end up blurting out something strange. "Are we friends? Because I can't always tell if someone wants to be friends with me."

"You can't tell even when they kiss you?" he asks, his tone gentle, patient, unconditional.

"Friends don't kiss." I gasp, looking up and finding that he's watching me intently. I knew he would be and I knew it would affect me this way. My breathing quickens and my heart pounds in my ears. "Oh. You don't want to be friends with me, do you?"

"Of course I do." Stephan looks a little confused. "Kit, why do you think I asked you out, and kissed you and put up with your dog licking my feet?"

"Oh, god, Bessie, stop doing that." I shove Bessie away from him, embarrassed that she's been doing that and I hadn't noticed, but Stephan just laughs.

"Define friends to me," he says, as he scratches Bessie behind her ears. "Just so we're on the same wavelength here."

I hesitate, because what is it that he's asking me to do? Talk about friendship, or talk about radio stations?

"I mean, tell me what you think we are to each other," Stephan clarifies helpfully. "And then I'll tell you what I think."

"You kissed me, and you asked me out." I twist my mouth a little as I ponder his question. "I think you want to be my boyfriend?" I make the statement into a question. "Or a hookup."

"A hookup?" Stephan exclaims. "No, Jesus, Kit, what the hell?"

"O-okay, sorry. I think I've messed this up and I haven't even given you the chocolates." I move away from him, but he doesn't let me leave go of his hand.

"Wait, you brought me chocolates?"

"Well, yes." I nod. "Yenta wanted me to bring you flowers because she thinks it's romantic, but flowers are technically dead as soon as you pick them, and giving someone something that's dead, when you really want them to get better, doesn't make any sense to me. So I went to the chocolatier's along the high street, even though it's not a day I usually go shopping, and asked the lady to pick some for you. Sorry if there are some you don't like. I wanted to call you to ask you which kind were your favourite but Yenta said that it would spoil the surprise."

As I speak, I take the wrapped box of chocolates from my bag and hand it to him, waiting for him to turn away, or to continue talking about what I said to upset him, but instead, he no longer looks angry. He looks, well, as if he's going to cry.

"You went shopping for chocolates, at a chocolate shop—even though you hate shopping and hate places like that because they smell—just for me?"

"Yes." I nod. "I mean, I don't hate shopping. It's just difficult." I grimace, worried that I'm oversharing again. "I only had to leave the shop twice while I was there. I explained to the lady that I might have to, and she was okay with it. She just chose a selection of her favourites. I hope you like them. Maybe we could talk about something else other than that boyfriend stuff because I think I made you angry, sorry."

"I'm not angry with you, Kit," Stephan tells me, still staring at the box of chocolates as if it is a thing of wonder. "I was just surprised that you might think I only wanted to hook up with you."

"So you don't?"

"No. I want to go out on dates with you. I want to get to know you. I want to spend time with you because I think you're lovely. And I do eventually want to be your boyfriend—if that's what you want."

"I think I want those things too." I nod, frowning as I concentrate. "There are some things we need to talk about."

"Can we talk about them over dinner? At Subway if that's where you really want to go."

"I—" I bite my lip, wondering if now is a good time to mention my alternative plan. The one I had meant to talk to him about yesterday when I found him in a ditch with a sprained ankle and it all went out of my head until I got home.

"Kit." Stephan grabs both of my hands and holds them tight, in that safe, secure way that has me breathless again. "If this dinner malarkey is too much for you, then we can do something else. Anything. I just want to spend time with you. I don't mind what we do."

"I—okay. I think I need more time to think." I don't, but I'm in danger of doing or saying something stupid and making a fool of myself. "You did say I could take all the time I needed. Did you mean that, or did you really mean you wanted me to give you an answer straightaway?"

"I meant it, Kit. Take all the time you need."

I nod, watching his face for what, I don't know, because I won't be able to guess what he's thinking anyway.

"I think I need to go now," I tell him. "I'll come back when I've thought."

"Of course." He smiles, squeezing my hand before letting it go. There is no hint that he is disappointed in any way, and it's not as if I've said no, because I haven't.

I stand up and he follows me with his eyes as I get ready to leave. Those eyes have me tied in knots, quite literally: my legs and arms refuse to move the way I want them to. Instead, in an impulsive move that is completely out of character, I reach out and touch his face with my fingertips. He gasps as I deliberately meet his gaze.

"Spring light," I whisper, before leaning in to kiss him. "I'll see you soon, Mr. Spring."

"I'll be waiting," Stephan whispers against my lips after laughing at the silly nickname.

I call to Bessie and she comes, following me out of the conservatory door and into the garden. I don't look back because I'm already thinking about my alternative plan for this date. I mean, I've already thought about it long enough. Why couldn't I talk to him about it just then? Why can't I go back right now? Will he think I'm odd?

Who am I kidding? He already thinks I'm odd. In fact, his entire family thinks I'm odd, and it doesn't seem to matter to them, or to him. I surely don't have anything to lose.

I look down at Bessie. "What do you think, Bessie? Should I go back now, just walk in there and tell him my plan?"

Bessie tips her head to one side, her ears twitching and her eyebrows flicking up and down.

"Urgh, you're no help. I wish you could speak."

I bite at my lip, flicking my thumbnails as I make my decision and burst back into the conservatory before I lose my nerve.

"I've thought about it," I blurt out a little louder than I'd intended.

Stephan looks pretty startled at my sudden reappearance.

"Bloody hell, mate, that was quick." The smirk that never quite leaves his mouth is firmly in place as he waits for me to continue.

"Yeah, sorry." I grimace. "I already had a plan, and I was going to tell you last night, but then I found you in a ditch, which was a bit unexpected, and then, today, I mean, just now, you had me all flustered, you know—" I wave my hands about in the general direction of my face "—the kissing stuff, and spaghetti Bolognese and toothpaste, and relationship statuses. It doesn't take much to get me flustered. I'm a bit of a dork when it comes to, you know, interacting with people."

Stephan is just looking at me with this massive smirk on his face. "Mate, you have got to be the most adorable dork I've ever met. I think you might just be practically perfect in every way."

"Oh, like Mary Poppins." I laugh then frown. "Except I'm not a nanny, and you're not a chimney sweep."

He chuckles. "Why don't you come back over here and tell me your plan? And while you're at it, explain the spaghetti Bolognese thing as well."

He pats the sofa beside him, and I do as he asks, sitting closer this time, so he doesn't have to shuffle over in order to hold my hand.

I take a deep breath and tell him my pizza plan.

Chapter Seven

Shopping for Pizzas
or
Why Do People Not Follow the Rules?

Today, I am shopping specifically for pizza ingredients for my date with Stephan. After I told him all about it, he agreed it was an awesome plan. I suspect he would have said that even if I'd suggested we go on a tour of the city sewers. That is something I'd quite like to do, actually. I'll have to write that down.

I want everything to be perfect tonight, so I have this shopping trip planned out meticulously. I really do like this man and want to make a positive impression after all the disastrous meetings over the last week and a half. He's already made a lasting impression on me. I know I will find it hard if he decides going out with me is too much of an effort.

I'm not hard work, just hard to fathom out. Stephan seems to have fathomed me out quite well so far. I just need tonight to go well and maybe there'll be some more kissing, perhaps something more than that, although that would indeed take a bit more planning and some understanding on his part.

Perhaps we'll talk about that some other time—if tonight goes okay, that is.

I live on the high street, right next to most of the shops I need to visit, but when any trip outside is fraught with the unpredictable, it's a good idea to have contingency plans in place for everything that could, or might happen. I packed the ones I need today in my backpack, just in case.

At the crossing, I wait patiently for the lights to change. Beside me is a woman with a baby in a pram. Beside her is a man smoking a cigarette. The smoke is blowing in the baby's face and the woman looks annoyed. It is rather rude of him, to say the least, and he doesn't seem aware that he is doing anything wrong. I find it very difficult not to point out these things when I come across them. Sometimes I wish I could just keep my mouth shut, but I really cannot help myself this time.

"You know, you shouldn't be doing that," I say, leaning a little over the pram so the smoking man knows I'm talking to him.

"Doing what, mate?" he asks, his voice gruff and gravelly enough to match his rough, tattooed arms.

"Smoking," I reply concisely.

"It's not illegal outside." He curls his lip and flicks the ash from his cigarette carelessly onto the ground. "Unless they changed the law when I wasn't lookin'."

"You're right, it's not illegal," I agree with him on that count, but still cannot let it go. "It's just that you're blowing your smoke in the baby's face and that's what I don't think you should be doing."

"Why don't you mind your own fucking business?" the man growls at me.

"Oh, that's a bit rude," I say, taking a step back. I don't think he'll do anything, because there's a pram in the way. Most people are a bit more accepting of my quirkiness, but this guy seems angry, which means he is actually very angry if even I can pick this up from his expression.

"He's telling the truth," the woman with the baby adds on my behalf, distracting the guy for a moment. "I really don't want your smoke in my baby's face."

The man gives her a long look, his lip curled in a sneer before looking back at me and stepping out onto the road. "Why don't you both just fuck off, eh?"

"Oh." I reach out to him as he steps out. "Wait, you shouldn't cross yet. It's not safe. The lights haven't changed."

"I can cross when I like, fucking weirdo," he growls back at me.

He takes a few more steps just as a car comes hurtling around the corner, horn honking as a warning. The guy jumps in shock and then makes a run for it, narrowly missing getting run over.

"Oh god," I gasp as I watch him turn and shake his fist at me and make obscene gestures at the driver of the car that just missed him. "He shouldn't have done that. He didn't follow the rules. Why don't people follow the rules?"

I'm not really asking anybody, but the woman beside me is laughing.

"He got his just desserts. That was rather funny, you have to admit."

"No, it was awful. He could have been killed." I feel a bit weak at the knees just thinking about it, and the fact that, because I know first aid, I might have had to do something about it if he had been hit, and after he was so horrible as well.

The lights change, but I freeze, because, although there are shops on both sides of the high street, the shops I want to go to are all on the other side and I don't much feel like crossing the road right now. Not when that horrible man is standing on the other side glaring at me like his mishap was all my fault.

I don't know what to do, because tonight can't happen if I don't get everything I need this afternoon.

"Are you all right?" the woman with the baby asks me. "Do you want me to call someone?"

Because of course she would come to that conclusion. I am rocking back and forth from my heels to my toes and flicking my fingers, muttering to myself like some sort of head case.

"No, no one thanks, I'm fine. I just need to…" I look around me for inspiration, a visual clue as to what I might have put in my contingency plan for getting out of situations like this.

– *Move away.*

That's a good plan. Move somewhere less—peopley.

I point ahead of me, towards a narrow alley between the shop buildings. Without looking in her direction I say, "I just need to go over there. Thank you for asking. Goodbye."

I make a rush for the alley. I don't look to see if she's watching me. I don't want to know.

Here, the sounds of the street are muffled. Today is not a particularly busy day, but even one person is one too many when I'm this close to losing my shit.

I lean back against the wall and take a moment to breathe. I can't cross the road. This is okay. I can just look at my contingency plan to see what my alternatives are.

I take my backpack off and swing it around to open it and get out my notebook. I wish Bessie was with me, but she isn't. I left her in the shop with Yenta for such a short, relatively simple shopping trip. It's easier than having to explain to every shopkeeper why she should be allowed into the shop with me. Most of them know she is my support dog, but some are funny about it. Besides, today I thought I'd be okay. How wrong was I about that?

Things would have been fine if that man had just followed the rules and not been so bloody angry about it when he almost got knocked over.

"Where's my bloody notebook?" I grumble as I rummage about in my bag.

Suddenly the bag is ripped from my hand, and I cry out as someone grabs my wrist and I'm pushed back against the wall.

"Think that was funny, did ya? What happened on the road back there?" It's the guy from the crossing. "Have a good laugh at my expense? Ya fucking weirdo."

I don't think he really wants answers to his questions. I struggle to get free, croaking out an apology that is so garbled it sounds like gibberish. I try to reach for my backpack, but he kicks it away and pushes me roughly up against the wall. I watch in despair as the contents of my bag are strewn across the lane.

"That's all my stuff." I gasp. "P-please let me go."

"God, you're such a spazz." The guy sneers. "I watched you pacing about like a loon. Leave yer carer at home, did ya? People like you shouldn't be allowed out in public. And where do you get off telling me what to do?"

"I've got as much right as you to be out anywhere I want," I croak at him, finally finding my voice because I'm angry now. He has no right to say those things to me. "I don't need a bloody carer, and I wasn't telling you what to do. I was reminding you of the rules."

"Yeah? Well, next time…" He leans in close, and his breath stinks. I turn my head but I can still smell it. He has bad teeth, but I don't think he'll appreciate me telling him about dental hygiene right now. I think he's already angry enough to hurt me. "Next time, keep your mouth shut and your thoughts to yourself. In fact—" his free hand grabs the front of my coat and twists the fabric until it tightens around my neck and nips the skin "—stay away from this part of the high street altogether, then you won't be bothering anyone. Understand?"

I nod as I pull at his hand to no avail. I've never been very strong even though I use the gym and stay fit. I feel panic start to set in, as it begins to get harder to breathe.

"Hey!" a voice calls from the end of the lane, and my attacker's grip loosens just a little bit. "Hey, what are you doing to him? Leave him alone, you bastard."

Oh god, it's Stephan. I don't want him to be hurt by this guy as well.

"What's it to you?" The guy lets me go and turns to face Stephan as he rushes into the alley. They meet chest-to-chest, their expressions dark and angry, and I'm afraid there'll be a fight.

Despite my throat burning and my shoulder feeling bruised where the guy had squeezed, I push between them, facing Stephan and looking up into his spring-light eyes that now look like a summer storm, flashing with thunder and lightning.

"Stephan, I'm fine. You can stop now. I'm not hurt. C-can we just go? P-please?" I want to run and not stop running until I get back to Yenta's shop, but I won't leave without him.

He's still glaring at the guy, his stormy eyes filled with anger and hatred.

"We're not the ones who should move on, Kit. He is." He leans past me and snarls at the guy. "Go on, get out of here before I do something you'll regret."

"You and who's army, then, pretty boy?" the guy hisses back.

Stephan smiles. I don't really think there's any reason to smile. No one said anything funny. I don't think it's a friendly smile, either. He holds up a clenched fist.

"I don't need an army," he growls. "I'm a Cassillis, and you'd better scoot before this connects with your face. You don't want to mess with me, mate, and you definitely don't want to mess with my boyfriend either."

The guy takes a step back, now looking unhappy rather than angry, and actually a little scared.

"Oh my god, a weirdo and a shirt lifter? I'm off, it might be catching."

Stephan takes another step forward, growling a warning, and the guy is gone before either of us can take another breath.

For a moment, Stephan stands very still, his fist clenched tight, before relaxing, his shoulders slumping.

"Jesus," he breathes as he turns to me and grabs me by the shoulders. His freckles are darker against his pale face. "Jesus, Kit, are you all right?" He takes a shaky breath. "When I saw that bloke with his hand on your throat, I saw red. What the hell was going on?"

"He was angry with me." I duck away from his hold and drop to the ground to retrieve my backpack and contents. He drops to his knees beside me, helping me to push things back into my bag but he's doing it in the wrong order. "Stephan, stop, let me do it myself."

"O-okay, I'm sorry." He moves back, but doesn't stand until I do, reaching out to support me when my legs threaten to give way. "Steady on, I've got you."

Again, I duck away from his touch. I can't process any of it right now. I need to find some way of calming down, but Bessie isn't here and my hands are shaking. I dig my fingernails into my palms, feeling the fog descend. I start to pace.

"I said something to him that I shouldn't have, except it wasn't bad. He wasn't following the rules. Why do people not follow the rules?" I'm gasping for breath now. "And now I want to go home, but I haven't finished my shopping, and I was shopping for stuff for tonight because I wanted it all to be perfect for you, and now it won't be."

"Kit, it's okay, mate. We can do the shopping together if you want, but I think you should sit down first, you're shaking like a leaf."

"Like a leaf. Like a leaf," I repeat his words like a mad parrot, jumping from one foot to the other as if I am a bird sitting on a perch. "No, no. I'm not a leaf and I can't sit, I mean, not here. I can't stay here. I need—I need—"

The words are stuck now as the world begins closing in around me. It feels like someone has put a sack over my head to stop me breathing. Things have got beyond the point where I can stop the panic. If I don't go home right now, I'm going to have a full-blown meltdown right here in the street, right in front of Stephan, and he won't want to be my boyfriend anymore and I only just found out that's what he thinks he is. Now he'll think the same as everyone else does: that I'm weird and I shouldn't be allowed out in public.

God.

"Kit." Stephan holds my shoulders again, trying to meet my gaze. His voice cuts through the fog like a beacon from a lighthouse, but it's too much, his touch, his concern, his kindness. I can't process it all. "Tell me what you need me to do," he says, and I know he wants to help, but I can't think about what I need when he's so close.

"Stop touching me," I yell, and his hands lift away from my shoulders as if they've been stung.

"I'm sorry, babe. I'm sorry. I won't touch you, but I'm not leaving. I'm not going anywhere. Tell me what else you need."

"I need…" I sob, trying to breathe and speak at the same time. "I need to go home. I need Bessie. I need…"

"Home. I can take you home. I can make sure you get there safely. Bessie will be there waiting for you, right?"

"She's always there for me. It's what she does." I'm clenching my fists so hard now I can feel my nails cutting into the flesh of my palms.

"Kit, you need to stop doing that, sweetheart. You're hurting yourself. Why don't you hold my hands instead?"

"I don't want to hurt you. I'm sorry I shouted at you, Stephan. You shouldn't be hurt. That man nearly hurt you, because of me. That shouldn't happen."

"No, that man hurt you because he's an arse. None of that was your fault, Kit, and if he'd hurt me, that wouldn't have been your fault either. Come on, let's get you home. Hold on to my hands, or anything, but please, stop clenching your fists. Your nails are cutting the skin."

I try to take some deep breaths. Through the fog, I hear Stephan's voice, soothing and pleading, and trying to make sense of what is going on. I have two choices right now: to carry on like this, getting more and more worked up, or let him help. I opt for the second choice. I hold onto his hands and let him guide me from the alley and across the street.

I don't look to see if people are staring. I close my eyes. Far from not wanting him to touch me, I find it is easier to tuck myself tight against his side, using him the same way I would use one of my blankets. I hope he doesn't mind. He wraps his arm around my shoulders and becomes a barrier between me and the rest of the world.

He keeps me safe until we reach the door of the bookshop.

"Oh my goodness, Lapushka!" Yenta gasps as we enter the shop.

I let Stephan explain what just happened. He does it quicker and more concisely than I ever would.

"Some guy attacked Kit in an alley, had his hands around his throat. If I hadn't turned up, I don't know what would have happened, Yenta."

"Oh no!" she cries, her hands on her cheeks. "Lapushka, are you hurt?"

Bessie is there, her head pushing up against my hands, letting me stroke her and calm myself down. As she does her thing, Stephan releases his hold on me but does not leave my side. Yenta steps to the other side and urges me to move.

"Come, let us get you upstairs. Stephan, will you take him up while I close the shop?"

Stephan guides me upstairs to my flat. This isn't how I'd planned for him to see my flat for the first time, but I'm now too tired to protest. I stumble to the sofa, grab a blanket and pull it over myself and Bessie, creating a safe, warm cave where the sounds of the outside world are muffled and distant.

"We should call the police," Stephan says from close by. Right now, it's like he's still a blanket, making the cave safer.

"No police," I mutter. "If the police come, I'll have to talk to them. I don't want to talk to anyone." I'm so drained I can't even lift my head. I rest it against Bessie and close my eyes, feeling her soft fur, breathing in her warm, spicy scent and loving her unconditional presence.

She's not the only unconditional presence, though, because I sense Stephan sitting close enough to touch, but keeping to himself. Waiting, always waiting.

How does he just know?

I peek from beneath the blanket. One of his hands is resting on the sofa beside me. Slowly, I reach out and place my hand alongside, my little finger tracing over his. The touch is gentle, but it doesn't hurt, not the way soft touch usually does. Without a word or even a glance in my direction, Stephan's little finger links with mine, and I feel a warmth travel up my hand and arm and fill my entire being.

Is this what it feels like? When you want to be with someone? It never felt like this with Harry. He never just sat beside me, waiting. Yenta is right, this feels different. But is it real? Will it last? Right now, he's here because he's worried, but once he knows I'm okay, will he leave?

Stephan and Yenta talk a little longer, in soft, quiet tones. I hear but I don't listen. It is probably about me, but it doesn't matter. All that matters right now, is that Bessie is doing her job and so is Stephan's presence. I am feeling more and more calm as the minutes pass.

"He usually sleeps after something like this happens," I hear Yenta say as the fog finally lifts and I can let myself listen again.

She has made tea. A peek from beneath my blanket cave tells me there's a cup waiting for me. I usually drink it cold anyway. I look to the side and see that Stephan is drinking his with his free hand, his other still occupied with mine, our little fingers still linked.

"Does it happen often?" Stephan sounds worried. "I mean, him getting attacked?"

"There have been incidents where people have lost their patience with him, raised their voice, called him names. He has never been physically attacked. This is awful, but a meltdown, he usually has one every two or three months. This was a bad one, but then, I think most people would react badly to being attacked like that."

"I'm sure. I sent the guy packing, but Kit should really report it to the police."

"Good luck persuading him to do that." Yenta's tone is now frustration. I recognise it because she gets frustrated with me quite a lot. "You might have noticed, but he finds it difficult speaking to people he's known for years. Think how he'll be when the police start asking him questions, and if he ever had to give evidence in a court? The prosecution would tear him apart."

"God, that's awful." Stephan sounds unhappy. "My dad's cousin does some things in a similar way to Kit. He's very different in other ways, though. He couldn't live on his own the way Kit does."

"Kit is his own person, Stephan. Autism affects everyone differently," Yenta tells him. "He likely has similar issues to your dad's cousin, yes, but he'll also be very different."

"Right."

I can't interpret Stephan's tone. He sounds unhappy, or maybe he's disgusted.

Well, that's it, I suppose. I never got to the stage where I had to tell him the reasons I do things the way I do. He knows now, and he's probably trying to think of an excuse to leave.

"I think he's amazing," Stephan whispers softly.

The words take a while to sink in, mostly because, at the same time, he moves his hand so that not only our little fingers are linked, but all our fingers are entwined. It feels like our entire beings have become joined and my hand is somehow part of him now. When his words finally register, they settle in my chest like something physical. My heart is beating so hard I'm certain he'll be able to hear it.

Some people talk about wanting to burst with excitement. I never really understood that until now, when I feel my heart will burst from my chest. I'd always thought it would be a horrible feeling, but it isn't. It's actually quite nice.

I suddenly want Yenta to leave because I want to be alone with Stephan. I want so much that it's all a bit scary.

As if he's somehow sensed what I'm thinking, Stephan urges Yenta to go back down into the shop, saying he will stay with me as long as I want him to. He does realise that could possibly be forever, doesn't he?

He sits back down beside me after letting Yenta out of the flat. He doesn't speak, as if he knows he has to wait for me to speak first.

I don't look up, my face still buried in Bessie's fur. "Did you push the top bolt right across the door?" I ask.

"Yes. Yenta showed me how to do it."

"I usually do that. It's always been me. I've never been here with anyone else except Bessie and Yenta."

"You can go and check if you want," Stephan says, his tone soft. "I won't be offended."

"That's okay. If Yenta showed you, then you'll have done it right." There's a moment of silence, and with Stephan, I know I don't have to fill it with chitchat. He just waits, like always. "You don't have to stay," I whisper, giving him the option to leave.

"I know I don't." He makes no attempt to touch me when I really want to be holding his hand again, melding our bodies into one. "But I will, unless you really, really want me to leave."

"I don't really, really want you to go anywhere," I confess. "But I know that some people find me hard to handle. Harry left because he couldn't cope."

"Well, Harry, whoever he is, is an arse."

"He was my boyfriend."

"Was he, indeed?" There's an edge to Stephan's voice that puzzles me enough to look up. I tip the blanket off my head to get a better look at his face.

Bessie takes that as an opportunity to leave me, her job done, and go and make a fuss of Stephan.

As he pets her and praises her for being a good dog, I study his face. Why did he sound so angry when I mentioned Harry? Was he jealous? I've never understood jealousy because I've never met anyone who felt it, nor have I felt it myself. I've read about it, but that's not enough to understand it.

"Are...are you jealous?" I ask him. "Why would you be jealous?"

He sighs as he continues to pet Bessie. "Don't worry, Kit, I'm not jealous, not really, just a bit envious that someone else got to call you his boyfriend, and we've never had any time to talk about us."

"But you are my boyfriend! You said so, to that guy, and you asked me if that was what I wanted to be the other night and I said yes."

Stephan smiles as his spring light eyes search my face.

"God, Kit, how could anyone ever want to hurt you? You're just—" His breath hitches, and I get the feeling that, if I let him, he would pull me into his lap and hold me in a tight embrace forever. "—perfect," he finishes.

"I don't know what you mean." I frown, looking away and staring at the floor. I want him to hold me, I do, but not just yet, it's too soon, and my body wants… It wouldn't just stop at a hug and Stephan doesn't want that, not yet. There are some things you have to do in the right order and I'm afraid I've got things terribly wrong. "I messed up our date. I didn't get everything I needed to make pizzas so now we can't eat together like you wanted."

"It's not always about what we want, Kit. What do you need to do right now?"

"Right now, I need to sleep," I say because I just want to hide away and shut out the world, especially if Stephan wants to leave.

"Okay." He nods slowly. "Why don't you go and have a sleep? Give me your shopping list and I'll get the rest of your shopping for you."

"Why would you do that?" I ask in shock. "I mean, I know I should say thank you."

"You're welcome, mate." Stephan smirks. He looks happy. I don't know why because now he's ended up doing the things I'm supposed to be doing. "I'm going to do your shopping so we can still have pizzas. Is that okay?"

"Yes."

"And is it still okay for me to come back and help you make them?"

"Yes. That too." I nod, still not really understanding why he even wants to do any of this.

"Where's your list?" he asks.

I produce it, pulling it from my backpack. I smooth it out before handing it to him. "S-sorry it got a bit crushed."

He stares at it, looking bewildered. "Gosh, I don't think I've ever seen such a detailed list."

"The actual list isn't that long," I explain. "The detail is there to remind me that it's okay if I can't get something specific and then I've sub-listed all the alternatives. It also has notes in the margins reminding me what to ask for and what to say to whoever is serving me and what they might say back. So I can, you know, have a normal conversation with them."

"Right." He's still studying the list like it's some sort of unfathomable user manual. I suppose it is in a way.

"If you ever wanted to understand exactly how I work, reading one of my lists will certainly help."

"You're not kidding." He chuckles. "When I get back, I think I might like to read some more of these lists of yours."

"I call them contingency plans. Do you really want to read them? Harry never did. He thought they were stupid."

"Harry is the one that was stupid if he didn't see these lists were as beautiful as the person who made them." He smiles at me before standing up and pressing a kiss to my forehead. "I really do want to read them," he assures me. "Now you go and have a sleep, mate, and I'll let myself out."

I think for a moment, getting it all sorted in my head. He waits for me to reply.

"Go out the back door, then I won't have to come down and push the bolt home. Get Yenta to let you back in, just in case I'm still asleep when you come back."

"Sure thing, if that's all okay with you." He seems a little unsure. I nod, smiling, not really needing to say anything more except I do. I need to check.

"You can just walk away, you know. You don't need to help me, or spend time with me or do anything with me. You've seen what I can be like. That wasn't an isolated incident, Stephan. It doesn't happen a lot, but I can't tell you it'll never happen again."

"Kit, I knew from the first moment I set eyes on you that no matter what, I wanted to get to know you. You should know that I don't scare easily and I'm not going anywhere."

"Yes, you are. You're going to the shops. You just said so."

He leans his forehead against mine, his hand on the back of my head giving just enough pressure for the touch to be pleasant.

"Oh, Kit." He sighs, kissing me quickly and leaving before I have even opened my eyes. "See you tonight, mate," he calls as he walks out of the room.

Chapter Eight

Pizzas Are Better When Shared
or
Grumpy Wake-up Calls Make
For Great Bedtime Reading

I SIT UP AND rub my eyes, disorientated because I don't usually sleep in the afternoon, or in my clothes.

I freeze as I hear a noise that seems to be coming from my kitchen. I glance down at the floor where Bessie usually sleeps. Yes, she's there, so whoever is in my kitchen is obviously not a burglar or an axe murderer. It could be Yenta, although she rarely comes into the flat. I doubt it is Stephan. He's long gone. I'm not expecting to see him again after this afternoon. I know he said he would do the rest of the shopping for our date, but he's surely had time to think things over and decide that being with me is too much like hard work.

There's another noise from the kitchen. Bessie doesn't even stir. She obviously doesn't see whoever it is as a threat, but for that to happen they'd only have to give her a dog chew, and not even an expensive, posh one. Just one of those twenty-for-a-pound ones that look like they've been made from compressed paper pulp. She's a cheap date.

"Bessie, who's here, then?" I ask like she's going to answer. She does lift her head, twitch her ears towards me, whine a little and then goes back to sleep. "Some guard dog you are." I huff, swinging my legs off the bed and standing, stretching out my muscles and yawning loudly.

"Kit, are you awake?" Stephan's voice calls from the kitchen, startling me and also giving me a warm feeling. This man continues to surprise me, in a good way.

I frown as I walk to my bedroom door and look through the living room to the kitchen beyond. Even though he's surprised me in a good way I still need time to readjust.

"What are you doing?" I ask after yawning again.

"Hello to you too." Stephan smiles at me as he leans against the kitchen doorframe, rubbing his hands on a tea towel he has tucked into his jeans pocket. Was he washing my dishes?

I scowl. I'm not at my best when I wake up. Especially when things aren't as they should be. I shouldn't be waking up now, because I shouldn't have been asleep. Stephan shouldn't be here for our date yet. He shouldn't be washing my dishes. All my plans have gone awry.

"You're here early." I scowl, grimacing when he just stares at me.

"I'm at a bit of a loss as to how to answer that, mate. You knew I was coming back as soon as I'd finished the shopping, right?"

"Yes, yes." I pinch my nose, nodding but still scowling. "I'm sorry. I mean, I felt the need to point it out, even though I know the reason why." I run my hands through my hair, which has become all tangled while I was asleep. I hate brushing my hair anyway, but having to do it twice in one day is just annoying. I get a bit caught up with the task of using my fingers instead of a hairbrush, scowling at a particularly stubborn knot at the end of a clump of hair. I tease it apart and click my tongue.

Stephan chuckles and I look up, still scowling, this time at him.

"Are you always this bloody adorable when you first wake up?" Stephan says, not making any attempt to approach me.

"If by adorable, you really mean grumpy and bad-tempered, then yes." I huff.

"I think I already told you I think your kind of grumpy is pretty damn adorable," he reminds me. "Is there anything you want me to do to make things a little easier? Go out and start again, maybe, or just disappear until you've sorted yourself out and got your plans in place?"

"No! I don't want you to disappear." I make a frustrated noise, giving him a sideways look. "You didn't mean that literally, did you?"

"No, mate, I'm not a magician." He grins. "You did say it was okay to ask Yenta to let me in while you were still asleep."

"I know, I remember now. Yes. I'm sorry for being a grump. I get like that when something is happening that I haven't planned for. Mostly, I just need time to readjust. Sometimes, rarely now, it ends in a meltdown like earlier. I'm sorry that you saw that."

"Kit, I was just glad I was there to help." He doesn't sound as if he's angry about it, or irritated. When I glance at him quickly, he's smiling. "I got everything on your list, just as you wrote it out. It's all here, ready for when you are." He waves his hands over in the direction of the kitchen bench where I can see pizza ingredients all set out and ready to go.

"Did you get the readymade bases?" I ask as I approach the kitchen. I can feel things falling into place now, getting back to where they are supposed to be in the order I had planned them.

He steps aside to allow me access to the bench. "Yes. The vacuum-packed thin crust ones from the deli, as you requested, m'lord." He executes an elegant bow and I narrow my eyes, liking the way he smirks at me but not ready to admit it yet because I'm still a bit grumpy.

Okay, not so much grumpy as disconcerted. I should be really bothered that he is in my kitchen moving my stuff around and basically making himself at home—I note the half-empty coffee cup—but it doesn't feel wrong. There's a rightness I can't explain and a warm feeling that I just don't understand. Well, I do, but this is a first date, so it's too soon to be feeling things like that, except, I felt them when he kissed me those two times at his hotel...and all the other times he's just managed to do and say everything right.

Instead of thinking about it too much, I choose to inspect the gathered ingredients. Not because I'm looking for flaws but because I need a distraction to stop me from pushing him up against the kitchen bench and having him right there and then like some sort of wanton hussy. There's an order to these things, and he makes me want to do it all in the wrong order.

He really has got everything on my list, exactly what I had written down. I feel my grumpiness dissipating like oil in water when you add a drop of soap.

"Okay, you've passed," I tell him. "Thank you."

"Aw, you didn't tell me this was a test." He pouts. "If I'd known, I would have studied harder."

His statement makes me laugh out loud, and he tips his head to one side as I lean back against the kitchen bench, feeling a little more at ease but not completely relaxed. Not yet. There are some things that need to be said. I push away from the bench, aware I've begun wringing my hands and deliberately not looking at him as I try, unsuccessfully, not to rock backwards and forwards on my feet.

"You probably have some questions. Yenta said you might have some questions."

"No more than I would normally have on a first date," Stephan replies.

That makes me look up, in surprise. "But our date hasn't started yet. The date shouldn't start until seven o'clock and it's only six-thirty."

"Well, then." Stephan is still smiling, and I can't tell if this is because he's happy, or amused, but at least he doesn't look annoyed or frustrated because of my pedantics over timing. "Maybe I should wait until seven before I ask any questions."

I frown, not really wanting to pursue the subject of this afternoon, but I think it might be better to get those questions out of the way before we talk about anything else.

"You don't want to talk about what happened earlier?" I ask, still not looking at him. I see from the corner of my eye that he is shrugging.

"Not unless you do," he says, surprising me again.

I regard him with my head tipped to one side, perplexed and disconcerted.

"I think I do. Need to talk. I mean. I think there are some things you should know about me. Things that might make or break this date."

"Kit." Stephan sounds shocked. "Mate, there is nothing you can say that will make me want to break this date. Understand?"

"Er, yes, I-I think so." I still can't look at him.

"I knew from the very first time we met that I wanted to get to know you better, and then, even after everything that's happened and especially after what happened this afternoon, I am willing to do anything I need to do to be part of your life."

"I don't need a carer," I blurt out, before he gets any ideas, or makes assumptions after what he witnessed.

"I-I'm not offering to be anyone's carer," he says, his expression serious as I watch him from behind a veil I've made of my hair, because looking at him directly will overload me with information.

"Right. Because I don't need a protector either. That's Bessie's job." I turn away, to look over all the pizza ingredients, rearranging them in the order they are supposed to be. "I can look after myself."

"I know you can." His tone is quiet and gentle.

"I don't need anyone to come and tell me that the things I do are wrong, or odd, or that I should be doing things I'm not."

"I would never do that."

"Because I had that. I made the mistake of allowing someone to take over, and—" I take a shaky breath "—it didn't end well. I mean, for me. I have no idea how it ended for him. I never saw him again."

"You're talking about Harry, aren't you?"

There's an edge to Stephan's voice that I don't understand. "Are you angry that I mentioned Harry, or angry that Harry hurt me?"

"That he hurt you, Kit, definitely. Not the other. Never the other."

"You will probably get angry with me at some point. I mean, people do get angry with each other, don't they? But they do with me in particular. It's just, if you are angry or upset with me, or with something I've said or done, or even something that I haven't said or done, you have to tell me. I'm not good at picking up on these things if you don't tell me. That was Harry's problem. He thought I should have been able to work out what I'd done wrong. He never did tell me why he left, in the end. He just—did."

"That's awful." Stephan's voice is very quiet, and I don't know if he's upset or shocked now. I think he might be both, because when I chance a direct look at his face, his eyes look a little red and his cheeks are pale.

"I don't want you to think that you have to stay out of some sort of obligation," I tell him.

"That's not why I'm here."

"Okay, so you need to tell me exactly why you're here, so that I will know for future reference."

Stephan nods, smiling and looking pretty calm, to be honest. He definitely doesn't look like someone who doesn't want to be here. I can at least hope he'll stay for the pizza. Maybe he'll even stay for me.

Stephan takes a deep breath and speaks. "I'm here because I think you are an amazing, brave, determined man and I hope that some of that determination might rub off on me, because I've never had to fight for anything in my life until I met you. And by god, Kit Winters, I'll fight for you to my last breath."

I let out a surprised huff of air and look up, fully meeting his gaze. "I-I don't want you to fight anything or anyone. I don't want you to be hurt."

"It's not that kind of fighting I'm talking about, Kit. What I mean is, I'm willing to put in the time and effort to learn what I need to."

I lean back against the kitchen bench as I watch him very carefully, my eyes narrowed.

"I think you already studied," I tell him. "You studied so well you should go to the top of the class, even though there's only one of you in the class and there isn't really a class or a teacher."

"Well…" He smirks as he takes a step closer to me. "I'm really flattered to be given such an accolade, but I really didn't study anything yet, Kit."

I click my tongue. He doesn't know everything he needs to, or maybe he does and he just skipped over some parts. Oh well, if he's willing to learn…

"Say my name first," I tell him, meeting his gaze for longer than I have since I met him.

"Eh?" He takes another step closer.

"I know it's inconvenient to try to learn a different way to speak to someone," I explain. "But when you say my name right at the end of a sentence, I tend to focus on that and not what you've said. If you say my name first, then you will have my undivided attention."

"Oh, I see." He smirks as he takes one more step, which brings him close enough to almost touch me.

I can feel his presence prickling across my skin, like silvery tingles of blue static. Any closer without pressing firmly against me and it will hurt, but he knows this. I know he does, and when he closes the gap, he doesn't caress me, he places his arms either side of the bench and crowds me, pushing me back with his body, firm and warm and hard against mine.

I look up at him, lost in those spring-light eyes, wanting to be lost forever, because he's beautiful.

He leans in close and whispers into my ear, "Kit."

"Yes, Stephan?" I whisper back, sliding my arms around his waist and pressing my hands over the muscles of his back.

"I think you are incredible and gorgeous."

"And now you have my undivided attention." I grin. "Although I still don't see how you can think that. I'm not the one that's gorgeous."

"Oh, shush." He chuckles. "You said my eyes were like spring."

"That's right." I nod, my breath quickening as his words send a rush of hot air across my earlobe and a pool of heat to my groin.

"If I'm spring, then you're summer. Your eyes are as green as a summer meadow."

"Oh." I really can't think of anything to say in reply, since no one has ever described me this way before. "I want to say I can't be summer, because my name's Winters, but I know that's just my pedantic brain working overtime."

"Kit Winters, I think your pedantic brain is a thing of wonder, just like the rest of you."

"And now I really do want to kiss you," I tell him. "I mean, not that I didn't before, but it was all happening out of order. But now, suddenly, it doesn't seem to matter because you make it all seem so safe."

"Oh, Kit." His cheeks are flushed pink as he turns his head just a little in order to kiss me, lips pressed firmly on mine.

With a moan, I push my tongue against his. He tastes warm, and right somehow. Everything about him is right. His smell, his taste, the way he just knows what to do and say.

When I pull away from the kiss, liking the way his warm breath feathers across my face, I keep my focus on his eyes. The eyes are the window to everything and often give me too much information so I feel overwhelmed and have to look away. Not this time. I want to be overwhelmed by him. I want to see.

"God." He breathes out the word as a soft sigh as the kiss ends. "Kit, you've got my insides tied in knots. Have done since the first moment I set eyes on you. I could fall hard for you, keep falling and never stop."

"Oh dear! You've already fallen into a ditch this week. I wouldn't want you to hurt yourself again," I say, trying to sound serious, but his mouth curls in a delighted smirk.

"You know I don't mean that literally, don't you?"

I grin. "Maybe."

"Definitely." He leans back in for another kiss and I go with the flow, because that's how this kind of thing works. If I think about it too much, I'll get swamped in the organisation, when really, my body knows exactly what it's doing and what it wants.

Right now, it wants Stephan Cassillis very much.

Stephan Cassillis's body, however, wants food, because his stomach picks this very moment to rumble very loudly.

"Oh dear." I pull back a little to regard his stomach before looking up into his eyes again. "I think maybe we should eat."

"Hey, good idea, and sorry." He grimaces. "That kind of killed the moment."

"Oh, don't worry about it." I pat his shoulder. "Makes a refreshing change for it not to be me."

"Kit, you don't kill the moments, mate, you make them."

***

Later, after we have made and eaten our pizzas, we sit together on the sofa. I'd quite like to do some more kissing, but before I can suggest it Bessie joins us from the bedroom and attempts to sit on Stephan's knee.

"I'll have to walk her soon." I comment, as Stephan manages to fend her off by scratching her ears.

"I can come with you if you want," he offers.

"Okay, as long as your ankle isn't hurting too much. I realise this is the first time I've mentioned it, and I know it's been a few days but hardly long enough for it to be fully better. I feel a bit bad about that."

"My ankle's fine, Kit. Light exercise is good, and don't worry about not mentioning it. You had other things on your mind."

"Okay."

We fall into a comfortable silence for a little while, and Stephan slides his arm around my shoulders as we sit. I shuffle a little closer, enjoying his warmth and the way he just knows how much pressure to use when he's holding me.

"As far as first dates go, this one has been quite nice," Stephan states.

I shrug. "I wouldn't know. This is the first first date I've ever been on."

"Really?" He turns a little so he can face me. "But you and Harry...?"

"We never dated." I shrug. "Harry moved in because he thought I needed him to, and I told you, I just let him take over."

"Oh." He returns to the relaxed position he was sitting in before he spoke, with Bessie sitting on the floor at his feet, her head resting on his knee.

He scratches her ear, a thoughtful expression on his face.

Would now be a good time to talk about the rest of the night? I've resisted so far because, well, when I talk about how much I've planned something, it can sometimes kill the moment, except, Stephan thinks I make the moments. Perhaps now is a good time.

"Stephan, can I ask you something?"

"I think you just did, mate." He smirks.

I click my tongue and shake my head. "Then can I ask you something after this?"

"Of course you can. You don't have to ask to ask."

"Oh, stop confusing me, doofus." I hit him with a cushion and he curls up in self-defence.

Bessie gets in on the act, finally seeing her chance to jump up onto Stephan's knee.

"Bessie, get down. You're ten tons of solid dog," Stephan complains, still trying to defend himself from my cushion assault as well as her tongue. "Okay, I yield."

"I yield?" I laugh, but stop hitting him. "Who says things like that anymore?"

"I do." He huffs, smoothing his dishevelled hair. "Right." He turns to smile at me. "What did you want to ask?"

"Are you planning on staying the night?"

His lips part, as if he is half in the act of saying something but he doesn't quite know what to say.

"Bloody hell, Kit. That was a bit direct and to the point."

"I'm sorry." I grimace. "I don't know any other way to be. I mean, I don't do subtle, and I don't do spontaneous. I mean, I need to have these things planned out. I don't like uncertainty.

It stresses me to the point, of, well, you saw what happened this afternoon."

"That was a pretty stressful situation. Anyone might have reacted the same way you did."

"I doubt that." I look away. How can he always manage to make even my worst behaviours seem so acceptable? "But are you? Staying the night, I mean?"

Stephan sits up a little straighter, clasping his hands in his lap as if he is nervous now.

"You don't have to," I tell him, trying to make him not nervous. "It's just, I need to know, so I can, you know, put all my plans into place for, you know…" I grimace as I wave my hands in the vague direction of the bedroom.

"You have contingency plans for sex?" Stephan gapes at me, and I hang my head, knowing I've gone too far this time. I mean, who the hell has contingency plans for sex? And worse still, who the hell tells their potential partner they have already planned out their first bedtime activities to the last letter? He'll be running for the door, screaming that I'm a loony…

"Mate, that is awesome." His smile is broad, and his eyes, when I chance a look, are dancing with spring-light.

Once again he has managed to surprise me. I stare at him in surprise as his smile broadens once more.

"Kit, I think I need to see those contingency plans, because I really would like to stay the night at some point, if that's what you want, but only if I'm absolutely sure I know enough not to mess this up, because I don't want to, you know, mess this up."

"Do you really want to see my contingency plans?" I regard him dubiously. "I mean, I think I already told you that Harry never wanted to. He thought they were stupid, especially the ones for bed."

"But the bedtime ones are the most important ones to get right." Stephan frowns. "How did he know what you liked if he didn't read them? Did you tell him?"

"I would try to, but it never worked out the same way. Sometimes I'd get in a bit of a muddle, and he would just get impatient with me and we would end up doing everything he wanted and very little of what I did. I mean most of the time it was fine, because it felt good but at the same time, it all felt a bit out of control. Not that I'm a control freak, because I'm not. That's not the reason I need to know what's happening next."

"Oh god." Stephan sounds a little upset now, and he looks a bit pale as he falls back into the sofa cushions, his hand across his mouth.

"Are you all right?" I could remind him about my first-aid training, but I don't think this is an appropriate time.

He recovers quickly, his smile returning as he gazes at me. "I'm fine, mate. Never better."

His words make me laugh and he tips his head to one side, smiling. "What's funny?" he asks.

"I like the way you say mate, that's all, and I like that it has several meanings, one of which, has…"

"Sexual connotations." He nods in understanding. "I get it. It also means friend."

"We're not friends, though, are we? We're boyfriends. At least, that's what you said. If you want to change that after tonight then that's fine, I don't mind. Eating pizza with a friend is still better than eating on my own."

"Kit." His hand presses down firmly on my leg. He always uses just the right amount of pressure. He is so good at remembering. "I still do want to be your boyfriend, but boyfriends can be friends too. In fact, it's much better if they are."

"Do you think so?"

"I know so, mate." He smiles at me, taking my hand in his and twining our fingers together. "Now, why don't you go and get those contingency plans and we'll read them together. I'm not saying we need to do anything with them just yet, because I'm in no hurry. I just want to make sure I get everything right when we do."

"I don't think you could possibly get anything wrong, Stephan. You've been on a roll since we first met."

He laughs and is still laughing when I return from my bedroom with my backpack full of notebooks and other important stuff.

"Ah, the infamous backpack." He chuckles.

"Infamous? It isn't the villain in a movie. It's just a backpack."

"Maybe, but it is important. And if it hadn't been for that backpack, I might not have followed you home that day at the library or learned your name or asked you out on a date."

"No. I suppose you're right." I stare down at the unassuming black bag. It doesn't seem possible for something so nondescript to have been so integral to Stephan and I getting together. "It wasn't just the backpack, of course. If Bessie hadn't crashed that wedding…" I leave the sentence hanging.

"Oh god, yes." Stephan chuckles. "I don't think anyone there that night will ever forget. My dad plays that CCTV footage over and over on a loop. He's still laughing about it."

"Oh dear. Now I feel I'm infamous, or Bessie."

"Not infamous, mate, just famous, amongst my family, anyway. Are these the contingency plans?" he asks as I hand him a stack of three books.

"Yes." I nod. "Well, these are the most important ones. I don't carry all of them around with me. There are rather a lot, and some of them are quite detailed."

"Yes, I remember your shopping list," Stephan muses as he studies the intricately decorated front cover of the first book. He runs his fingers over the designs. "Did you draw these? They're beautiful."

"They're just scribbles," I tell him, surprised he could think they were anything else. "Sometimes I doodle when I'm thinking."

"You could sell these designs. People would love them."

"Bollocks." I laugh out loud. "Surely no one would want to pay money for my scribbles."

"I think they would." Stephan shrugs. His hand hesitates before he opens the first book and he looks up at me. "May I?"

He's about to delve deeper into my world than anyone, even Yenta, has gone. She sometimes helps me write the contingency plans, but she has never read one herself. With a little trepidation,

I nod. He said he was willing to do anything to be part of my life, and these plans are a big part of who I am and how I make sense of the world.

I watch as he reads, first one book then the next. The ones about shopping and walking Bessie; about having conversations and waiting for others to have their say. The ones about friendships, and how not to be an arse when someone is trying to be nice to me. I still need to do a bit of work on that one. And finally, he reads the one about being intimate. I try not to squirm.

"I haven't quite finished that one," I explain. "It all got a bit too graphic and I had to take a break."

"You're not kidding," Stephan whispers as he closes the book and holds it in his lap, his eyes wide and his cheeks a little flushed. "I can see why you had to take a break, mate."

For a moment, he just sits there, staring at nothing, probably deep in thought. It's a lot to take in all at once. When he does eventually speak, his voice is quiet, subdued even.

"What would your contingency plan be if someone told you that they love you?" he asks, not meeting my eye, staring down at the notebook in his hand, his finger tracing slowly over the designs I have drawn on the cover.

I think for a little while and I get the sense that Stephan is holding his breath.

"Love is a big word," I begin, still thinking. "I mean, technically, it's a small word, only four letters, but it takes up a big space in your head." I take a shaky breath. "And your heart." This is getting into territory I didn't really want to cross right now. Love is not a subject I feel I can speak of with any confidence. I don't understand emotions at the best of times, but when they are expressed and not meant... "No one should ever say it," I whisper, "unless they really, really mean it."

"Is that your rule?" Stephan looks up from the book but he does not leave go of it, holding it tight as if his life depended on it.

"Not just mine. It should be everyone's rule. But I..." I take a deep breath and sigh. Why are we talking about this? Would it be appropriate to try and change the subject? I don't want to get all flustered and upset in front of him, but if he pursues this, I will.

"Someone said it to you," he states before I can think of anything to say as a diversion. "And didn't mean it?"

I nod. "Yes."

"Was it Harry?"

"Yes," I say, my voice getting quieter with each question.

"Tell me," he urges, his voice gentle and caring.

"He said he loved me, and then he said I wasn't what he wanted. But if I wasn't, why would he say he loved me? When you say something like that, it means you'll stay forever, so he can't have meant it, because he left. I don't always understand how other people feel. I mean, I'm not very good at guessing how they feel, but I'm not an emotionless android. I can relate if the person talks to me and explains how they're feeling. If he was unhappy, he should have said, but he never did, and when he left…" I take another deep breath, because this is where it gets most difficult and where I have to explain a little more about myself than I really wanted to share right at this moment… "I find it hard enough to deal with small changes. Big changes are even harder to accept. When he left, it was one change too many?"

"Too many? What do you mean?"

"Six weeks before he left, my mum died."

"Oh god." Stephan's face goes very pale. "That's awful."

"I don't remember a great deal about those weeks. I know Harry found it very hard to deal with the fact that I was really not dealing with anything at all. So he left me to not-deal with it all by myself. If it hadn't been for Yenta, I might have ended up homeless on the streets—in hospital, even. I think I was very close to being committed."

"Really? You seem pretty sane to me."

"Perhaps now. But then…" I wiggle my hand "…not so much."

"And Harry, he never came back?"

"No. He did try to call me, but I never could hold a decent conversation on the phone. He took that to mean I didn't want to speak to him and that I hadn't actually felt anything for him at all in the two years we'd been together. You probably guessed that there's a lot of things I'm not very good at. And it's not from lack of trying. It's just the way my brain works."

"But there's an equal amount of things you are very good at, Kit. In some cases, you're an expert, judging by the content of these books." He points to the one in his hand and gives me a rather candid look, flicking his eyebrows. "I think I need a lot more practice at some of these things, with an expert as my tutor."

"Oh, you mean first aid, obviously," I say with a slight smirk because I know he really means sex. He snorts.

"Er, no, not quite, but there are healing qualities to the other activities."

He's quiet for a little while and then he speaks again.

"I think we touched on a very heavy subject just now."

"Weight has nothing to do with it, but yes, it is a difficult thing to talk about. Harry said he loved me, and I thought I loved him, but perhaps I didn't, because I didn't really miss him, once I'd got over the initial shock and the antidepressants started to work. I miss my mum, but not him. Perhaps that's just me, not understanding any of it. Perhaps I'm not even capable of feeling the same as other people."

"Kit, your feelings are no less relevant just because you experience them in a different way. Besides, this Harry was the emotional numpty. I've said this before, but it bears saying again: Harry is an arse."

"Right." I don't really want to talk about Harry anymore, so I change the subject and hope he doesn't mind. "Going back to your original question, about contingency plans. Do you think I might need one?"

"I think you might need one very soon," he says, the spring-light hovering in his eyes as he meets my gaze.

"Oh," I whisper, swallowing hard. "I don't really know what to say now, because I don't think I'm ready to say it back. It's the wrong time, and the wrong order. There are things we need to do before either of us says anything like that."

"I know." He nods. "I understand now that I've read these." He pats the books on his knee before turning to face me so he's sitting sideways on the sofa. "Kit, I'm going to make you a deal."

"I... Okay. Deals are things I understand really well since I have a degree in business studies."

"Bloody hell, really?" His mouth opens wide in shock.

"Don't sound so surprised."

"I'm not surprised because you have a degree, Kit. That's brilliant, but you and I are going to have to work on our information sharing, you know, so you don't drop any more bombshells when I'm trying to focus on something else entirely."

"You're the one who mentioned some sort of deal," I remind him. "So my statement was relevant."

"Okay, okay." He chuckles, holding his hands up in surrender.

I wait, but I'm not as patient as Stephan, so I speak before he's ready. "Well, come on, then, what's this deal?"

He regards me with narrowed eyes before taking a breath to speak.

"I won't say that big-little word until I'm sure that you've got a contingency plan ready, and definitely not until I am absolutely certain, without a doubt, that I will never ever leave."

"Right." There he goes again, knowing just exactly what to say and telling me he'll wait without him ever being told he has to. But how long is he willing to wait this time? "What if it takes me forever to make my plan?"

"Then I'll wait forever, Kit. I'm not planning on doing anything else, or going anywhere. I'll be right here waiting."

"And what if it takes until the next time we have a springful of winters? That could be decades."

"Then that's how long I'll wait, my lovely, lovely boy." He holds out his arms for me to decide whether or not I want to be held. I do this time. Perhaps I will every time with him, because he makes it all so unconditional.

"Not a boy, remember?" I remind him, as I snuggle into his side, feeling safer there than I ever did anywhere else. Stephan's arms wrap tightly around me, holding me in his warm, safe cocoon. "But thank you, Stephan. I think you're lovely too, and I think I shall enjoy this forever business."

"Oh Kit, me too."

The End

Well, not really the end; it's actually just the beginning. I mean, sometimes people write 'the end' and they don't mean that it's the end of the story, just the end of what they're willing to write.

"Kit, mate, come to bed." Stephan calls from the bedroom, sounding uncharacteristically impatient.

"Okay Stephan, don't have a cow."

I don't mean that literally. I don't think he's really going to have a cow if I don't come to bed right now.

"Mate, who are you talking to?"

"No one, Stephan, just my contingency plan notebook for dealing with boyfriends who snore."

"I do not snore."

"You don't have to listen to it. Believe me, you snore."

**Really The End or I do actually believe
Stephan will have a cow.**

Author's Note

Kit has Asperger syndrome, which is an autism spectrum disorder. Autistic people experience the world in a very different way to other people. They have specific difficulties with social interaction and communication. They can also have some sensory processing difficulties, which means they could have higher sensitivities to smells, tastes, touch, light and noise.

There are currently around 700,000 autistic people in the UK. That is more than 1 in 100. The condition does tend to affect men more than women, although we are slowly beginning to understand that women's autism presents in far more subtle ways than men's.

Kit's wish, if you will remember, was to write a manual to help people to understand him and be a little more accepting of his differences. It is the wish of most who are affected by autism that the wider world becomes more aware of the difficulties that they face every day. A little more knowledge and understanding equals a lot more acceptance.

For those of you who would like to know more about autism, or have in some way been affected by the issues explored in this book, here are some links that might be helpful.

https://www.autism.org.uk

https://community.autism.org.uk/f/adults-on-the-autistic-spectrum

https://www.autism-society.org

http://www.autismeurope.org

Autism charities around the world:
https://www.autism.org.uk/services/helplines/outside-uk/round-world.aspx

Autism Network International:
https://www.autismnetworkinternational.org

Assistance dogs:
http://www.assistancedogs.org.uk

YouTube currently has a wealth of information on autism, with many people sharing their own experiences with Asperger syndrome and autism spectrum disorders through video blogs. One such 'vlog' is Aspie World, which, along with others, was one I watched quite a lot while writing this story, and that, along with my own experiences, both professionally and personally, helped me a great deal when trying to put myself in Kit's shoes (even though I don't think they would actually fit me).

https://www.youtube.com/user/AspieWorld1

About Seasons of Love

Love follows no rules. Like sun in winter and rain in summer, love can blossom in the most unexpected places. This richly diverse collection of stories proves that love is as universal and as varied as the seasons.

The Stories:

- *Tourist Season* – Deven Balsam
- *Machete Betty and the Office Sharks* – Neptune Flowers
- *Once Around Seven* – Ofelia Gränd
- *Winter Blossoms* – Paul Iasevoli
- *Year of the Guilty Soul* – A.M. Leibowitz
- *The Great Village Bun Fight* – Debbie McGowan
- *A Springful of Winters* – Dawn Sister
- *Out of Season* – Bob Stone
- *Seashell Voices* – Alexis Woods
- *Courting Light* – A. Zukowski

Available as a complete anthology (ebook/paperback) and as individual stories (ebook + longer stories in paperback).

For more information/purchase links, visit:
www.beatentrackpublishing.com/SeasonsofLove

About Dawn Sister

Dawn is from the North East of England. Her life is spent juggling. The juggling balls are: children, husband, work (occasionally), voluntary work, professional knitting (notice she doesn't class this as work), and writing. When she has time she actually sleeps. The whole point of writing for Dawn is just to get it all off her chest and out of her head. If she doesn't write it down then she ends up having long conversations with the characters out loud and her husband thinks she's crazy.

Contact & Media

Twitter: www.twitter.com/dawnsister1

Tumblr: dawnsister.tumblr.com

Facebook: www.facebook.com/DawnSister

Goodreads: www.goodreads.com/DawnSister

Beaten Track: www.beatentrackpublishing.com/dawnsister

By Dawn Sister

Dazzled By The Light
The Halloween Incident
See You Smile (Love's Landscapes)
*Merry F***cking Christmas*
Eagle Man and Mr Hawk (Love is an Open Road)
Not a Word (Love is an Open Road)
Locked in the Moment (Love Unlocked)
A Springful of Winters (Seasons of Love)

Beaten Track Publishing

For more titles from Beaten Track Publishing,
please visit our website:

http://www.beatentrackpublishing.com

Thanks for reading!